THE GOVERNESS GAMBLE

A novella to
The Duchess Society Series

BY

TRACY SUMNER

The Governess Gamble by Tracy Sumner

Published by WOLF Publishing UG

Copyright © 2022 Tracy Sumner
Text by Tracy Sumner
Edited by Chris Hall
Cover Art by Victoria Cooper
Paperback ISBN: 978-3-98536-082-6
Hard Cover ISBN: 978-3-98536-083-3
Ebook ISBN: 978-3-98536-081-9

WOLF Publishing - This is us:

Two sisters, two personalities.. But only one big love!

Diving into a world of dreams..
    ...Romance, heartfelt emotions, lovable and witty characters, some humor, and some mystery! Because we want it all! Historical Romance at its best!

Visit our website to learn all about us, our authors and books!

Sign up to our mailing list to receive first hand information on new releases, freebies and promotions as well as exclusive giveaways and sneak-peeks!

WWW.WOLF-PUBLISHING.COM

Also by Tracy Sumner

The Duchess Society Series

The DUCHESS SOCIETY is a steamy new Regency-era series. Come along for a scandalous ride with the incorrigible ladies of the Duchess Society as they tame the wicked rogues of London! Second chance, marriage of convenience, enemies to lovers, forbidden love, passion, scandal, ROMANCE.

If you enjoy depraved dukes, erstwhile earls and sexy scoundrels, untamed bluestockings and rebellious society misses, the DUCHESS SOCIETY is the series for you!

#1 The Brazen Bluestocking

#2 The Scandalous Vixen

#3 The Wicked Wallflower

#4 One Wedding and an Earl (coming January 2023)

More to Follow!

Prequel to the series: The Ice Duchess

Christmas novella: The Governess Gamble

THE GOVERNESS GAMBLE

If I could but know his heart, everything would become easy.
-Marianne Dashwood, *Sense and Sensibility*

Chapter One

Where Our Heroine Becomes an Accidental Governess

A Warm Parlor in a Cold Country
Limehouse, December 1823

Of all the salons in London, he had to walk into hers.

Although he didn't notice her.

Which wasn't a surprise as she wasn't noticeable.

Francine Shaw recorded Lord Remington's brazen entrance, recognition rolling through her like a wave off the ocean she'd crossed to get to this grit-choked city. During her time in England, almost six months now, he was the only man who had sparked her interest.

A fascination that ticked upward each time she'd seen him.

A notorious libertine who didn't even know her name.

While Franny's job, according to her father, was to attract a destitute nobleman, not a rake, and unite centuries of English nobility with her family's common-yet-prosperous lineage.

Two unremarkable people in an unremarkable world.

An unremarkable marriage but a solid business venture.

Franny grimaced behind her gloved hand, recognizing the irony. She was *exactly* as expected. A covetous American in want of a title. While William Allerton, fourth or fifth Viscount Remington, she couldn't recall without consulting *Debrett's*, was exactly as expected as well. A handsome scoundrel fighting to retain his masculine liberties while protecting a legacy he feasibly hadn't wanted in the first place. She'd heard the story numerous times batted about society parlors like a ball. No one in London seemed to have the funds to maintain the burdens they'd inherited.

In America, most inherited nothing and fought for *everything*.

As the viscount crossed the room, Franny tucked herself tighter into the recessed alcove, her back butting the chilled windowpanes overlooking the Thames. She peeked around the velvet drape, perfectly content to hide during this exchange. *Damn and blast*, she vowed, her heart giving a hard kick. Lord Remington looked as delectable as ever. Stylish but not flawless. Sturdily rumpled. Dark hair in relaxed disarray. Tall and trim, with an athletic grace few men in society could claim.

She sighed softly, giving her hands a tremulous clench. Thankfully, the echoes of ships banging the dock and the shouts of stevedores unloading crates funneled inside her nook, hiding any sound she might make. Interestingly enough, at least to Franny, Mrs. Hildegard Streeter, recently married to Mr. Tobias Streeter, rogue king of the Limehouse docks or so the scandal sheets claimed, occasionally chose to conduct business from her husband's rookery warehouse.

Today that business was with Franny. In a vibrant, vile neighborhood her father would faint upon learning she'd agreed to visit.

This morning had been the most exhilarating Franny had experienced in months. Which said much about her state of boredom *and* her predisposition for trouble.

"You've got to help me," Lord Remington said, his first words spoken, the casualness of the statement detailing a startlingly close relationship with Mrs. Streeter. The viscount didn't stop until he practically bumped the desk Hildy sat behind with his lean hip, casting a twisted grin her way, charm he was renowned for.

He was taller than Franny had realized, a shade too thin perhaps. But with broad shoulders and chiseled features one didn't easily forget. Something apart from his physical gifts, however, captured her attention. Lurking beneath his careless smile was serious intent. Even, possibly, a hint of vulnerability.

Franny wasn't the only woman enthralled. He'd been known to dance not a set, yet leave the ballroom with the most beautiful woman in attendance.

Hildy, perhaps the most stunning creature in England, calmly placed her quill beside her folio, her brow winging high. Daughter of an earl who had married a smuggler-cum-architect for an improbable love the likes of which London had never seen, she had it all. Had what Franny *wanted*. Aspirations considered silly on this side of the ocean, and the one she claimed across the way.

For once, England and America were in agreement.

Wishing to be someone's once-in-a-lifetime anything was pointless —when marriage was a business. She'd been raised by a father who believed in nothing *but* business.

Love had never factored into the equation, not once.

Bringing Franny from her musing, Mrs. Streeter laughed and smoothed her hand across the desk, her elegance truly admirable when Franny recognized the defiant personality buried beneath. "Chance, you're coming to me, oh, about a year sooner than expected. But I did expect it."

Chance. Franny pressed her palm to her belly, her cheeks heating. *Chance.*

Remington choked out a groan and dropped into the chair across from Hildy. Hooking a boot certain to be Hoby on his opposite knee, he drummed a silent tune on his thigh. "Oh, *no*. No matchmaking, Hild. No Countess Society or whatever it is you've got going. I need help, but not that kind." His smile dimmed, the song on his thigh going silent. "Not yet, anyway."

"We're not matchmakers," Hildy murmured. Although in a roundabout way, they were. She and the Duchess of Markham, Georgiana Munro, had created the Duchess Society with the thought to empower women on the cusp of marriage. Review of marital contracts and placement in a union not solely benefitting the husband. In the course of business, matchmaking had occurred even if Hildy and Georgie preferred to lightly conceal this fact. Their endeavors also included investigation into prospective partners, which is why Franny was there. Men in want of a wife often lied about their circumstances. Franny's father had someone he thought would make an adequate husband. *Adequate* was all he was shooting for. A baron he wanted to ensure wasn't in worse financial trouble than he'd stated.

Remington dropped his head back, his gaze crawling to the ceiling. Franny drank him in like brandy, drawing the strong line of his stubbled jaw on her palm. He had a crook at the top of his nose from some misadventure. Her fingertips itched to sketch him. The pad of paper and pencil hidden away in her spencer's pocket fairly shouted to be released. "You've made quite an exceptional life for yourself, Hild. Queen to the rogue king, the two of you ruling Limehouse. If I hadn't seen you together, I'd likely never believe it myself."

Hildy's cheeks pinkened as they did when anyone brought up her husband, Tobias. Her love, a glow that radiated like a flame to brighten the room. "Enough flattery, Chance, out with it."

"I've got a problem," he finally said, his voice sullen. Swiping a thick strand the color of charcoal from his brow, he slid lower in the chair. "An immense one."

Hildy rearranged a folio on her desk, patience personified. "Is it Arthur?"

Remington grunted softly and yanked again at his hair. It was longer than current style dictated, the locks snaking around his slim fingers like a vine, dusting the edge of his collar. He'd apparently left his hat in his carriage because Franny could see an indentation where it had recently sat on his head. "Unbelievably, my brother has managed to remain at Cambridge for the term. I negotiated a settlement of sorts for the brawl in the Wren Library. It's been around since the 1600s, so they're fairly protective of the place. As if the crumbling roof on the estate in Hampshire wasn't enough to deal with.

"Tenants in Derbyshire are set to revolt after the way my father left things. The townhouse in Berkeley Square is not in the grandest condition, either. This title is killing me. If not for my side project, and your husband's valued partnership, I'd be in appalling financial shape like the rest of the *ton*. My dipping my toe in trade sickens them but saves *me*. For the moment."

Hildy braced her palm on the desk and rose. Strolling to the stack of crates serving as a mock sideboard, she shot Franny a fast look and brushed her index finger across her lips—*quiet*. A command Franny was exceedingly happy to follow. "You know Toby and I are more than willing to assist if you need a loan. I've known you since we were children, Chance. There aren't many friendships I value, but yours is one of them. My mother even said, if we traced our lines back far enough, we'd find we were cousins."

"Well, Cousin, my solicitors have informed me that I have a ward. A little girl. Six years old. Her father was my uncle, a distant relation three times removed or something. He left the care of her to my father, so she now falls to me along with the rest. When I've never even had a sister to look after. Only one unruly brother. I'm vastly out of my element here."

Hildy popped the tumbler to the sideboard, thankfully cutting off the sound of Franny's gasp. "A ward?"

"Hence my frantic need for a governess."

Hildy lifted the glass she'd likely intended for Remington and took a stunned sip. "You have frantic need of a *wife*."

Massaging the bridge of his nose, Remington closed his eyes. Franny couldn't determine their color from this distance. And she'd never been close enough to see. "I'm begging you. Through Christmastide. A fortnight. In the new year, I'll secure a proper arrangement."

"You've pedaled through a dozen mistresses. Ask one of them. The Duchess Society does not supply governesses. Or wives, for that matter."

"Bloody *hell*." Remington shoved from the chair and strode to her, snatching the glass from her hand and polishing off the contents. "Consider this a familial favor, Hild. One measly governess for a well-mannered urchin. How hard an ask is that for your society magicians? I'll pay as well as I'm able. And I'm a deuced congenial employer." This said, he unleashed a smile that crinkled the skin around his eyes, a smile that Franny felt to her toes and back. While his cousin seemed unaffected.

"Don't waste your charm on me, Chance Allerton." But she was grinning when she said it. It was confirmed then. No woman could resist the man. "Or should I now call you Lord Remington?"

The viscount's shoulders slumped, a weary sigh leaking forth. "You'll help me."

Hildy wiggled the glass from his hand. "I'll help you. But only through the holiday. A fortnight. Then you must find a permanent solution. I have two children, two felines, and a growing business to care for without worrying about you. And Arthur. And now this poor, orphaned girl."

Crossing the room, Remington halted by the door. "I must be off. I'm leaving to retrieve the girl. Then I'll be at the Derbyshire estate, which may or may not be overrun by irate tenants. I'm fairly certain it *won't* be by servants. I think my funds only employ three. I'll send a carriage round for the governess you locate on Friday. Is that enough time?" Knowing he'd won the battle, he leaned recklessly against the doorjamb, his good humor returning. His reputation for masterfully blending gallantry with a cagey hunger that drew women like cats to cream was well deserved. "I thank you from the bottom of my battered heart, Hildy."

"I'll figure something out, as I always do." Hildy tapped her knuckle on her bottom lip. "We'll be at Hampton Hall for the holiday, so I'll pop over and check on things next week. Lord Grimley is holding a ball, too. I'm assuming you were invited, along with everyone in Derbyshire."

Remington grumbled, his delight fading. Titled men were sought-after properties, even the impoverished ones, eliciting what amounted to female skirmishes on ballroom floors. She'd witnessed more than one from her frequent spot behind a fern or column.

Hildy settled the glass on the sideboard and turned to him. "The governess I send you, she's not to be dallied with, Chance."

A hint of temper sparked in his form. He straightened from his slouch, offended. "Message delivered, Hildy. You have my word. With the thousands of mistresses I apparently have, who needs a governess?"

6

Then he tipped his head and was gone, his footfalls ringing off the scuffed planks outside Hildy's makeshift office. A brother's exit, almost rude but acceptable, again proving how close they were.

Franny stepped from behind the drape, her nerve endings tingling. She looked to find Mrs. Streeter gazing at her with a concerned expression.

"Not like any viscount you've ever seen, is he, Miss Shaw? Arrogance and helplessness wrapped in silk. What a captivating combination, and he probably doesn't even realize why."

"I'll do it."

Mrs. Streeter stumbled over a wrinkle in the Aubusson, the only graceless move Franny had ever seen her make. "Do *what*? You're here to review agreements my solicitors have preemptively drawn up for Baron Hillsdale. This tangle with Remington"—she slashed her hand through the air as if she held a wand—"has nothing to do with you. If not for my affection for the man and my appreciation of his dire situation, it would have nothing to do with me. But as you can see, he's like family, so..."

Franny shrugged and dragged her slippered toe across a silver thread in the carpet. "I haven't agreed to Hillsdale," she said in a tone that sounded less amenable than it should when she understood her fate perfectly. Her father had threatened to cut her off should she refuse to marry. "This governess gamble isn't the worst proposal unless you have someone else in mind. Lord Remington is desperate, and I'm educated fairly well for a woman. My father believed in tutors, even for a girl. I'm without any plans for the holiday, as Papa is on a ship bound for New York as we speak. A strike in one of his plants. I'm an American outcast, but perhaps this won't make much difference to a reprobate viscount in need of assistance. I can sketch the days away while helping with this girl. I like children. Strangely enough, although I have no siblings, I'm quite good with them."

And I want to sketch Lord Remington more than I want my next breath. But I need to be close enough to him to do it.

Mrs. Streeter groaned and slumped into the chair behind her desk. "Your father has requested we investigate details of the baron's situation, so he's certain of this association even if you're not. Hillsdale swears on his mother's health his debt is not worse than he's admitted. When what he's admitted is not good. He has a penchant for gaming hells without any talent to support his passion. The bright spot is, he seems rather timid around women. Therefore, there aren't any he's *keeping* if you get my meaning."

Franny strolled to the chair Lord Remington had vacated and casually settled into it as if she wasn't seeking a trace of his heat. His scent. The air smelled faintly of raw wood and leather. Her heart gave a frightening kick. "Then trust his information is accurate, as the baron is *very* attached to his mother."

Mrs. Streeter chewed on her lip. "I can talk to your father. Give you more time perhaps to meet someone—"

Franny interrupted with a flick of her hand. "If not Hillsdale, Papa will decide on someone else. At least the baron is young and rather attractive. If you fancy bashful, light-haired men of small stature. You're going to factor my return to Philadelphia into the contracts. Should I choose to do that. This leaves me room to maneuver when I wouldn't have otherwise had that. It's my dowry he's after, not my person."

"At some point, the baron will want an heir, Miss Shaw. It's more than money with English society."

Franny glanced at the ceiling, searching for what the viscount had seen. Nothing but a tiny spider crack near the corner and row upon row of industrial crimson pipes running the length of the space. Mrs. Streeter's husband, Tobias, was an architect, in addition to an entrepreneur and distillery owner. A philanthropist. All this from a half-Romani who had crawled from the gutter to sit atop a kingdom. Coming from a country that valued the common man building an empire, Franny found this extremely impressive.

She could tell Mrs. Streeter she was aware of a wife's marital responsibilities. Aware, too, of what a physical relationship with a man entailed. She'd made a colossal mistake a year ago that had started her father down the path of seeking a marriage for his daughter, far from scandal. An idea orbiting wildly among affluent circles in Philadelphia. Purchasing a blue-blooded Brit was becoming fashionable when Franny had never been a fashionable girl.

She could also tell Mrs. Streeter she'd seen Viscount Remington exactly three times before today.

The first had snagged her like a hook beneath her skin. A musicale at an earl's townhouse, a name she couldn't recall on a day she could barely remember. She'd only been invited because her father and the earl were discussing an investment in railways in the north. She'd been hiding on the terrace, her small sketch pad balanced on the marble balustrade when she'd heard sounds rippling through the open window at her side. The click of a door, a heavy tread, a whispered sigh of appreciation. She'd leaned to peer inside, expecting to find a couple embracing.

Which would have brightened up a dreary evening considerably.

Instead, she'd found Viscount Remington crouched before an ornate bureau the English loved to call an escritoire. She'd watched in utter fascination as he ran his hand along the fine-grained rosewood, his lips parted in admiration. He had long, slim fingers better suited to a pianist. It'd been the first time—the first *true* instance—when she identified raw desire coursing through her body. A yearning so fierce it weakened her knees. She'd had to brace her hand on the balustrade to support herself.

This instance had brought to light her absolute foolishness in a murky parlor in Philadelphia. That had been nothing compared to this. Mere curiosity she'd ruined herself over.

When she'd looked back through the window, Viscount Remington had been gone.

He'd not once glanced at her that night. Or the other two times she'd seen him on the streets of London.

If she accepted this phony governess assignment, he'd have to.

"I'm frightened of the rapture on your face, Miss Shaw. Lord Remington is a complicated man, and his reputation is less than desirable. Women and wood are his main pleasures in life."

Franny huffed a startled laugh, her gaze seeking Mrs. Streeter's. "Wood?"

"If you follow through with this outrageous idea, you'll find out, anyway. He designs furniture."

Franny blinked, her curiosity growing. The scent of raw wood *had* invaded the space with him, which now made sense.

"A hobby that has grown to be more than a hobby. Although the *ton* has no idea, even if they're sitting in a chair he created. My husband and his partner, Xander Macauley, ship Lord Remington's pieces and act as cover for the business. It wouldn't do for a viscount to be openly involved in trade. Tobias even has a desk of Remington's in his study." For some reason, Mrs. Streeter's cheeks flushed at this declaration. "He's incredibly gifted. And conflicted because his talent isn't valued and likely never will be. His father was not kind, to start. His childhood wasn't a happy one."

Happy and childhood didn't belong in the same sentence. At least they hadn't belonged in Franny's sentence.

"Miss Shaw, let me be clear. I love Remington dearly, but I wouldn't want my sister, if I had one, to set her cap for him."

"I'm not setting my cap for anyone." The idea was ludicrous. She was plain. Bookish. She *looked* like a governess. Tightly wound as a clock, according to her companion, Ada, who had been with her since Franny's mother passed when she was three. Her ability to sketch was the only remarkable thing about Francine Shaw.

And her eyes. They were a rather dazzling shade of gold. But that was it.

Furthermore, she was plump when current fashion preferred reed-slim. Her hair was as badly behaved as she was, bursts of amber streaking through the curly, brown strands, feral unless she severely contained it. She even had a scattering of freckles across her cheeks. Her accent was a flat-voweled atrocity the English found vulgar. It was certain no man would offer for her that wasn't being paid to.

"Then there's the matter of your notoriety at the moment. Your father has been vocal about his hopes for you at every event he's attended. Public discourse the Duchess Society wouldn't advise, but it's too late. Unless he's been living under a rock, Lord Remington will recognize you the moment you step into his home. The moment you say one word."

"Simply tell him I've come from America and need employment. A pet project of the Duchess Society or some such. Distant relation of one of your husband's shipping partners. Lord Remington won't recognize me. I'm invisible to men like him."

Mrs. Streeter stilled, her lips parting in astonishment. "Miss Shaw, shy isn't unattractive. It may dim the blaze, but it doesn't expunge it. You're lovely and unique. It's a perilous combination."

Franny waved the comment away, unaccepting. "I'll tell my father I've been invited to a winter house party at the country estate of a viscount. Through your introduction, of course. The opportunity for encounters with titled men of modest means. Ada will hate it, but she hates everything about England. I can't change that. In any case, how challenging can one little girl and a cantankerous viscount be?" Franny crossed her fingers in the folds of her skirt, the lie rolling off her tongue like honey. "I'm only suggesting it because I have nothing better to do, and your cousin needs assistance."

Mrs. Streeter shook her head woefully. "Fine. I'll arrange it. Your last hurrah before marriage to the scant-statured baron. If your companion sticks to you like glue, and you avoid Remington as often as possible, perhaps nothing will go awry. Our home in Derbyshire is only a twenty-minute carriage ride away, should you need me."

Franny sat back with a smile, her plan in motion. She might like the country, she decided, future sketches of Chance Allerton swimming through her mind.

An orphan. An outcast. A tortured artist.

What could possibly go awry?

Chapter Two

Where a Fatigued Viscount Ponders Parenthood

Three Days Later at a Viscount's Shabby Estate

Chance threw his booted feet atop a desk in the Allerton family for two centuries and dropped his head to his hands. His skin smelled of nutmeg and chalk. He had a dab of what he hoped like hell was jam on his sleeve. He'd run circles around the house without a hint of pleasure surrounding the effort.

It was two hours past twilight, and he'd just gotten the girl to bed.

Katherine Elise Brierly, a six-year-old termagant and his problem for the rest of his *life*, wasn't well-mannered as he'd promised Hildy. She was the most talkative creature he'd ever had the misfortune to meet. She had opinions on every topic, many suited to a woman, not a child. How his cravat was tied. His boots polished. The ragged trim on her counterpane. The tattered velvet drapes in her bedchamber. The water stains on the ceiling in the breakfast room.

Chance groaned and massaged his temples.

And the *questions*. How old was the estate? How big? Did he have horses? Why was his majordomo, Alfred, so crooked? Was he married? Did he plan to be? Did he have a dog? Perhaps kittens? The girl had stated unequivocally that she wanted kittens.

Chance glanced across the space, considering the drink cart without thought to make that wish happen.

Raising a child was a damned sight harder than it looked.

He'd found himself explaining things he could—his marital state, number of horses and pets—and leaving much of the rest to his house-keeper, Mrs. Walker. Who let him know right off she couldn't keep up with a child without the assistance of the governess variety. His father had, somewhere along the way, let Rose Hill's staff go due to dwindling funds, so they had the bare minimum. Although he'd not spent much time in Derbyshire growing up, Chance recalled Mrs. Walker being around *forever*. She was likely as old as this desk.

Despite it all, however, he liked it here. Miserable memories from his childhood weren't a part of this place.

Lifting his head, he gazed about at what had once been an impres-sive library. His father had sold off many of the volumes, leaving gaps on dusty shelves. Cobwebs. Streaked windowpanes. Faded carpets. General neglect, which his father had excelled at. With regard to dwellings and children.

But the foundation was solid. Like a sliver of wood that would make a gorgeous piece of furniture once he took it in hand, he knew, with hard work and an infusion of capital, he could restore the estate to some level of its former glory. There was a dowager's cottage at the edge of the woodland that would make an astounding workshop. He currently leased space in London from Xander Macauley, his shipping partner, which worked out well enough.

But this would be *his*.

It all came down to blunt he didn't have. Time he wasn't sure he could allocate when he had two *other* decaying properties to worry about. A brother in the middle of a dangerous rebellion. A thriving business, his passion. When aside from making furniture, he'd never had a passion. No woman he couldn't live without, that was certain.

He recalled the smile on Hildy's face the other day. He wanted what she had with Tobias Streeter. He truly did. Society assumed because he played fast and loose that he didn't wish for a wife, a family. He might be a scoundrel, but he was *not* a cad. Of all his affairs, none had ended, except for the one with that fanatical countess, with a vase being thrown at his head. He was friends with each and every chit he'd tupped. His predicament was more, well, he'd never needed anyone enough to *fight* for them. Or had never felt he could *let* himself need anyone might be the best way to describe his quandary.

Now this girl. Katherine Elise Brierly. Six-year-old hellion in muslin.

Was *she* the peculiar start to his family?

Chance drifted to sleep dreaming of off-limits governesses and talkative girls who tugged his heartstrings.

***

Viscount Remington's eyes were blue.

A piercing, haunting blue. She likened the color to the icy glints shimmering in the snowflakes swirling about. One caught on the bow of his top lip and melted while she watched, setting her knees trembling beneath more layers than she'd ever needed to wear in Philadelphia.

Alas, her shivers were not due to the brutal English winter.

His expression stunned, Remington halted in the entranceway, her portmanteau dangling from his fingers. The coachman who had accompanied her was seeing to the carriage and horses, arranging for her trunk to be delivered to her bedchamber. Her companion, Ada, stood to the side of the corridor in disparaging silence, which was as it should be. Ada was unhappy about arriving four hours late due to the storm and even *more* unhappy to be plotting a governess farce in this "blasted wreck of a country."

"You're American," Remington said, his gaze racing the length of her as if he searched for a mark to verify his evaluation.

Flustered, Franny gathered her woolen spencer at her neck and trundled into the house, shutting the door behind her with a creaking slam. Her skin was chilled to the bone, but her cheeks were hot. "And you're a viscount who answers his own door."

He laughed, a husky surprise to the three souls huddled in the foyer of a medieval structure in obvious need of love. And heaping piles of money, Franny surmised as she gazed around.

The dwelling dazzled, nonetheless, make no mistake.

Although she'd come to sketch the man, the viscount's fortress would do in a pinch. From the ancient gatehouse at the end of the winding drive to the acres of winter-lush forest wrapped like a cloak around the estate. Towering chimney stacks rising from the snow-laden mist. A trench surrounding the house she thought could properly be called a moat. It was like nothing *she'd* ever seen. A castle straight out of the fairytales Ada had read to her when she was a child.

Remington gestured to the barren hallway. "The few servants I have are abed. My majordomo is as aged as the planks beneath our feet. He rarely makes it past sunset. Our housekeeper, Mrs. Walker, is much the same. I'm afraid it's left to me to escort you to your chamber. We're rather informal in the country."

Informal meaning impoverished. The funds needed to fully staff such a monstrous place were not available. Franny glanced over the viscount's shoulder, down the arched gallery, to the grand staircase spiraling to opposite wings of the house. Except for being wealthier than almost everyone in London, she could be Cinderella. Stepping away from her staid life for one night of adventure. Or two weeks, rather.

When she looked back, it was to find that the viscount's gaze had followed hers down the hall. From his scowl, it appeared that what she considered magnificent, he considered a burden.

"It needs work," he muttered, his chest lifting with his deep inhalation.

"It's lovely, my lord," she countered, her fingertips giving a familiar tingle, yearning to sketch. His vexed expression was nothing short of enchanting. "Majestic. Stately, even. We have nothing like this in Philadelphia. And in your family for centuries. How remarkable. My home is less than ten years old." She shrugged. "Everything in America is new."

Ada grunted and scrubbed her thumb over the scuffed oak paneling that was likely two hundred years old, obviously preferring new.

Remington took his time returning his attention to Franny. His thorough review revealed his effort to see the dwelling as she had. A considerate, unexpected response. His lashes were long and dark, dusting his skin as he blinked. His shirt and buckskins were damp at the hem and cuff, as if he'd recently returned from outdoors. He wore an unbuttoned gray waistcoat, his cravat untied and hanging loosely from his neck. No coat. Sleeves rolled to show an indecent amount of muscled forearm. He ran his palm over his unshaven cheek in contemplation, his jaw flexing with thoughts he kept to himself.

This was not the flippant lord the *ton* whispered about.

Hildy's words rang in her mind. *Doesn't look like any viscount you've ever seen, does he?*

No, he did not. It's why, from first glance, she'd been intrigued. Intrigued enough to lie about being a governess and wedging her foot inside his castle door.

The most appalling in a life of appalling decisions.

Franny's heart skipped a beat as she stared at him. Men never listened. No one who looked like him anyway, sly beauty and winsome charm. Franny spoke without expecting anyone to. The men who listened, listened because her dowry was big enough to solve their problems and nothing more.

"The well-mannered girl I promised Hildegard Streeter is a terror," he said when his gaze finally met hers. His eyes were the color of hydrangea petals, even more glorious in milky candlelight than they'd been in full moonlight. "She assured me in her letter that you're experienced enough to handle it. The chit has a thousand questions for which I have no answer. She wants biscuits and milk every other minute. Her threshold for boredom is the lowest I've encountered in another living soul." He cocked a broad shoulder and chewed on his lip, the one the snowflake had melted on. "I don't have sisters, and I don't know how to talk to girls."

Franny covered her mouth with the back of her hand, but too late.

Her laughter rolled like a carpet between them. *Not know how to talk to girls, indeed.*

Then, there it was.

A flash of temper she would wager a hundred English shillings, or half crowns, or whatever the coin the British preferred to wager was not an emotion William Allerton, fifth Viscount Remington—she'd looked it up in *Debrett's*—often exhibited to the masses. A cross turn of his mouth she was *determined* to capture with her charcoals.

"A lot written about me in the rags is rubbish, Miss..."

"Shaw. Francine Shaw," Franny replied, certain he wouldn't know who she was. Giving a false name was more of a charade than she was willing to construct. She didn't like lying even if she was moderately gifted. Strolling down the hallway, she noted the vaulted ceiling rising three stories, the balconied floors leading off the central staircase bordered by imposing balustrades and chipped sculptures. Faded carpets, tattered velvet drapes, threadbare furnishings. Ancient stone and marble. It was shabby but glorious. "The story about an opera singer leaving the stage to kiss you in full view of a slew of patrons is slanderous drivel then?"

"*Miss*," Ada hissed, striving to dictate what a proper lady would do when she was only guessing herself. They both knew it was a waste of time. Franny was hopelessly improper in every way. In America *and* England.

Remington froze, her luggage bumping his muscular thigh. Some mysteriously masculine scent drifted from him. Spicy, perhaps citrus. This overruled only by the dour odor of spearmint. On more than one occasion, her companion's stinging fragrance had arrived before her, notice Franny had used to her advantage. "That was the Duke of Leighton, who was sitting to my right. It was *his* box. Of course, they attribute the mischief to me. His Grace has the foulest temperament in London and a *worse* reputation but somehow gets aways with everything. It's the damned duke privilege."

She'd heard about the Duke of Leighton's antics. Why, he'd recently gotten tossed in the Thames by Xander Macauley. The men traveled in a pack, Viscount Remington an oft-time contributor in their escapades. "I'm teasing," she finally said when he didn't seem to understand that she was.

Remington frowned, tiny grooves radiating from his eyes. He looked bewildered; the kind of bemused charm Franny imagined his paramours overlooked. "That must be an American pursuit. We English never, *ever* tease. Especially governesses. My tutors were dry as cedar. Smacked my knuckles with a ruler while expecting absolute obedience. The number of broken ones, rulers, that is, during those years was enough to make my father weep."

She tilted her head, imagining how she was going to draw that lank of hair on the side of his head that kicked out a bit. She'd noticed it on two occasions now. "I don't think that will be my approach."

Remington grimaced. "You haven't met the girl."

Franny grinned. She couldn't help it. She had two weeks to explore this monstrous medieval fortress and the complexities of a man she found fascinating. She'd brought enough charcoals for a hundred sketches. Plus, she loved children.

Truly, what an adventure.

Ada coughed from somewhere behind her, the scent of spearmint clinging to the air.

Catching her companion's response, Remington eyed Franny with curious intent. "Why are you so delighted?"

Franny dragged her sodden slipper across the frayed carpet, working to erase her smile. "Christmastide is just around the corner." Although there wasn't one hint of cheer about the place.

He snorted, a dimple flaring in his cheek. How maddeningly handsome he was. It was unjust.

"This fascinating position as governess?"

He shifted her portmanteau to his other hand and flexed his fingers like he was working out a cramp. "Try again."

"My un-English nature?" she said with a laugh. A foxed baronet had told her it was the most sensual of sounds after he'd cornered her behind a settee at the countess's dinner party last week. She'd eventually had to bring her heel down on his instep to get him to move away from her person, but she'd been flattered, nonetheless.

Remington tried his best but, in the end, laughed with her. His fist going to his mouth to cover it. "That must be it." Then, he shook himself from his reverie and jogged up the staircase, her gaze left with nothing to do but record his trim bottom shifting in meticulously fitted buckskins. He must have forgotten the adage, ladies first.

But then again, she was no lady.

Ada hooked her arm through Franny's and tugged her up the stairs. "Stop it. I can see those scalding glances a mile away," she whispered, thankfully so low only Franny heard. "Flirting and your feeble inability to tame your base attractions is what landed us on this horrid side of the ocean. If I have to drink another cup of tea..."

"I'm not flirting. I'm talking to my employer. And what woman doesn't have base attractions? Isn't it normal to appreciate art? A fine form? Men are surely allowed this weakness."

Ada sighed wearily. "Heaven help me, should your father find out about this scheme. Daughter of one of the wealthiest men in Pennsylvania acting as a servant. The girl who went through a governess a week herself. When he does, it's off to live with my brother and his wife in Dyberry. You'd do that to me when I changed your nappies? Wiped your nose and darned your stockings? Covered for you that time you snuck in the window after dark with blackberry brambles in your hair? Dyberry is my pension, is that it? Why, it's in the country, and you know I have allergies!"

Franny drew Ada close. She was the only mother Franny had ever known. The only parent she'd *needed*. Her father certainly hadn't been up for the job. "You're going to change my children's nappies someday. Where I go, you go. How could I live without you?"

Ada sniffed. "Are you sure, Franny darling? After all that happened last spring?"

Her breath tight, Franny paused at the top of the staircase, noting that the shabbiness continued on this floor. Not even half of the lamps were lit. Dour paintings covered the walls, their frames coated in dust. Tattered carpets in worse shape than those on the main floor. The sconce's glow struck the viscount's broad back as he continued down the hallway, in and out of shadow, unaware they weren't following.

She didn't want to think about that night ever again.

Sliding her arm from Ada's, she sucked regret back through her teeth. "It's very simple. I won't let Gerald ruin me."

Any more than he already had.

Her reputation was one thing, her happiness quite another. She would die before letting him take more from her.

Ada twisted her gloved fingers in the folds of her skirt. "The English aren't forgiving. I could tell this right off. The way they gossip at these parties we've been forced to attend, it's more of a lashing than high society back home ever thought to give. Should the scandal reach this side of the ocean, your father's money won't be enough to buy a cobbler, much less that baron he has lined up. Women aren't allowed the mistakes men are, not in this world, not in any world. I wish you'd get that through your lovely but thick head."

Franny watched the viscount halt before a door at the end of the corridor, his long body hidden in shadow. When he turned to her, his eyes glimmering in a flicker of candlelight, she made a promise.

Two weeks. To play this harmless game in a hidden locale where she might be able to take a full breath for the first time in years.

She didn't deserve more. She didn't deserve *love*.

She'd written the ending of her book during one fateful encounter.

After this impulsive respite, she would marry the baron who wanted her money—and follow society's rules.

Every last one of them.

Chapter Three

Where a Forlorn Heiress Finds a Friend

F ranny guessed it might be easier to connect with a lonely child when you'd *been* a lonely child.

In some ways was still one. Or rather, a lonely woman.

Taking a deep breath, she entered the playroom as if she belonged there. She'd traveled the hallways, passing dozens of parlors and snaking warrens before finally locating the chamber. Katherine Brierly perched on the window seat, gazing at the snow falling in feathery wisps outside. She was thin, tall for her age, her disheveled hair shot through with red-gold sparks much like the crimson threads running through the threadbare carpet at her feet. Her stockings were tattered, her dress rumpled. She looked like an urchin but held the stately bearing of a queen.

Franny had been warned by the housekeeper, Mrs. Walker, that the ginger coloring matched the girl's temperament. She'd laughed when Mrs. Walker said it, eliciting a smile and an extra biscuit on her plate at breakfast. Franny had found that the English domestics were surprised when they were treated as *people*.

"Hello," Franny said as she crossed the threshold. The room smelled like the rest of the house, of dust and if not decay, disuse. There were scant books and toys on the shelves. Landscape paintings unsuited to a playroom lined the walls. The wallpaper faded and of scenes no child would want to see. Franny made a mental note to send to London for supplies the viscount could likely not afford but couldn't reject, either, once they'd arrived. Already paid for. Better to ask for forgiveness than permission, she'd always thought.

Katherine swiveled on her seat, the second-view of the child's face before she drew it into recalcitrant lines.

She was lonesome. And frightened.

Franny made a decision then and there. This girl's happiness added to the list that included her own. "We build snowmen at home," she said and moved into the chamber. "Although we don't often get enough to make a truly good one. I never had anyone to help me, so I got very skilled at making them myself."

Katherine swallowed, her apple-green eyes widening with interest. "Snowmen?"

Franny laughed and strolled into the room as if this interview wasn't of great importance. Love or hate, the battle lines drawn in moments with children, she'd found. "Not something you can do in the city, is it?" She crossed to the window and gave the chilled pane a hard tap. "This snow looks fluffy. So, it may be a challenge. Are you up to it?"

Katherine slithered from the window seat, her lips forming a half-smile. "You want to go outside? In the snow? Right now?"

Franny shrugged. "You can't build a snowman inside the house."

Katherine took a step closer, her hands twisting in her skirts. "We'll get wet."

"Probably, yes."

"Our hair messy," she challenged and drew a lazy loop around her head. "Our clothes drenched. We'll look like we've been pulled through a keyhole."

"Uh-huh."

"I don't have boots."

Franny sent a sweeping glance around the playroom. "We can locate something."

"Not very ladylike," Katherine whispered, reaching to pull her braid between her teeth. "But Americans aren't ladylike, are they?"

"We're not known for it. I'm certainly not." Through the window, Franny searched the distance, marveling at the parklands stretching as far as she could see. A rolling vista gorgeous enough to take one's breath. This estate was in need of care, true, but the terrain surrounding it was amazingly beautiful. "We'll get holly and pine to decorate while we're at it."

Katherine turned from her search of a wardrobe tucked in the corner. She had a boot in her hand that looked fifty years old. "For what?"

"Why, Christmas, of course."

The child's gaze shuttered. "The viscount won't like that."

Franny rested her hip on the window ledge, entering delicate territory. "Whyever not?"

"He doesn't like me," she said, chewing on her braid. "He prefers calm and order. Like my uncle. Then he died, and now I'm here. In another dreary household with another dreary man."

Franny traced a sketch of a bluebird on the wall, her gaze leaving Katherine. Sometimes falsehoods were hard to issue while staring into someone's eyes. "Lord Remington has great responsibility resting on his shoulders with his viscountcy. And he has no sisters, no children, so this is very new to him. *You* are new to him. But that doesn't mean he doesn't want you. He's likely to start building his family soon, and you're a part of that now."

"Are you my new governess?" Katherine's brow scrunched curiously, her braid dropping from her teeth. "You don't look like any governess I've ever seen."

Franny grinned, delighted. "I am. You may call me Miss Shaw. I'm here until Lord Remington can secure someone properly English. I'm a friend of his friend and in need of companionship during Christmastide. My father returned to America, and I truly had nowhere to go. My companion, Ada, loves the season and will help us decorate."

This could not be further from the truth. Ada had never met a length of garland she wished to hang nor a present she wished to wrap.

Katherine plopped to the floor and wrestled the boot on her foot. "You were drawing in the parlor after breakfast."

"That's my favorite hobby in the world. I've been sketching since I was your age."

"Can you teach me? I don't have anything I know how to do well."

Franny felt a surge of affection, fierce in its power. "I can."

Katherine giggled and reached for the other boot, finally looking like a little girl set to go on an adventure. "Miss Shaw, since we're becoming friends, you may call me Kat."

***

Chance couldn't tear his gaze from the enchanting scene outside the library window.

Katherine and his new governess, Miss Shaw, were building a lopsided snowman on the sloping lawn across the way. It was going to tumble if they put too much weight on the top portion. He'd been waiting for it to tumble. Ten minutes earlier, he'd watched them gather pine branches and holly from an overgrown thicket near the side garden, frolicking about as if it wasn't cold as a witch's teat this morn.

They had to be soaked to the skin. Clothing sodden, fingers and toes numb.

Nevertheless, they looked rapturous. The first time he'd seen this emotion from either of them.

He wanted to ignore the enchantment of the scene but couldn't.

As was often the way with life, he was toasty from a blazing hearth fire, his belly full of tea and toast—yet he was melancholy for some reason.

"You shouldn't have come without alerting me," he murmured to Lady Chapman-Holmes as she wiggled into the nook between his body and the wall. "I have the girl to think of now."

Eleanor snaked her arm through his, leaning into him. "How was I to know you'd been burdened with a child to care for? As if anyone would consider you father material. I'm staying down the way at Lady Dane's as we discussed last month. A ten-minute carriage ride. I'll see you at Grimley's ball in any case. Remington, I didn't want to unduly surprise you. I simply wanted to *see* you. One of the benefits of being a widow, I can travel alone on occasion."

Chance withdrew his arm as politely as he could. Eleanor wanted to stake her claim is what she wanted. As she'd wanted in London, to his discontent.

It was his fault, the direction his life had taken. He'd once desired her. Or women like her. Desired a different piece every night if he could manage it, in fact. And in his youth, he had. Champagne sipped from slippers. Or navels. Tangled sheets one moment and awkward silence the next. Interactions lasting only as long as his release.

Truly, he'd only been passionate about designing furniture.

He glanced back to the girls romping in the snow.

Something was happening, a mysterious yearning. He rubbed his chest, his breath catching. His existence was changing in the seconds being counted off on the mantel clock behind him. He felt powerless and *powerful*. On the precipice.

Lady Chapman-Holmes was situated in his old life.

When he suspected he was preparing for his new.

"What are they doing?" she asked, her tone scathing. "I assume the little one is the urchin you're now guardian of."

Enjoying life, he thought dully, suddenly determined to follow Miss Shaw's improper lead. At breakfast, she'd chatted with every servant who had stumbled into the morning parlor. Which due to his meager finances, amounted to four. Chance was charmed by her nonchalant playfulness. The joy she took in the blueberry jam she claimed was the best she'd had since leaving Philadelphia. The delicate teacup she claimed must have been in his family for years. Mrs. Walker's grandson, the scullery maid's brother. She asked about them all.

She was unlike any woman he'd ever met in that she didn't seem bothered by what people thought of her. When he'd been raised by an indifferent man who believed in basing his entire *being* on what people thought of him. Chance recalled being hugged exactly once by Viscount Remington. At his mother's funeral.

His father had never made any dwelling feel like *home*.

In the two days his temporary governess had been in residence at Rose Hill, there were changes he could only attribute to her. Feminine touches. The dank hallways smelled faintly of lemon and linseed oil. The paneling in the foyer glistened. The scent of biscuits—nutmeg and cinnamon—wafted down the gallery and into the space he'd set up as his workshop. More sconces were lit on the corridors he traveled. The drapes were open in rooms once deserted, letting in sunlight and life.

When he noticed Miss Shaw and her charge gathering up their pine branches and sad bits of holly to return to the house, he shoved off the window ledge. "You must go," he said and propelled Lady Chapman-Holmes across the parlor with a hand at her lower back.

Suddenly, he didn't want his old life to meet his new.

But the collision was inevitable.

Miss Shaw was opening the door as his majordomo was nowhere in sight, her bonnet a soggy mess hanging half off her head, her hair curling wildly about her face. She had insanely beautiful hair, so thick pins could scarcely contain it. A mass of mahogany and auburn, he'd been tempted since the moment they met to tunnel his fingers through. And her eyes... they were a remarkable shade so light they looked almost gold. He'd glanced at them twice across his breakfast table to confirm the assessment.

Lastly, and he hated to contemplate the notion with a former lover standing by his side, but his governess had the most delectable body of any chit in England. In Europe. In America. A voluptuous, petite package he longed to unwrap. Almost perfect from the little he'd seen of it.

Curve upon curve upon curve.

While he stood there lost in lusty reflection, Katherine barreled in behind Miss Shaw, her arms full of branches. "Franny," she called before she saw him. Because if the child had seen him first, her joy would have shriveled like the branches in her arms were soon going to. "We'll place these greens on every hearth in the house. It'll look like Christmastide then!"

Franny. He rolled the name across his tongue like a fine Bordeaux.

His governess spun in a circle, her merriment illuminating the foyer like a thousand candles. Happiness this house had not seen in years. Happiness he'd *never* seen.

Chance knew it was a ridiculous flight of fancy, but part of his heart raced away from him at that moment. A gut punch he felt to his toes. Greedy, he wanted to snatch her joy and light his soul with it.

Eleanor glanced at him, noting his stillness, her lips pursing into a severe pout. He couldn't stop her before she leaned in and busked his cheek, lingering in a manner that spoke of extreme familiarity.

Franny and Katherine quieted, believing they were intruding.

"My lord," Franny murmured, her cheeks coloring. Her wisp of a stunning smile dying. Her gaze darted between him and Eleanor. "Come, Kat, let's go organize our decorations. Excuse us, please."

Then she was down the gallery and up the stairs, Katherine-who-apparently-preferred-to-be-called Kat's footfalls tapping against marble as she raced alongside her.

Eleanor turned to him in a fury. "Why is that uncouth title-chaser in your home, Remington? She didn't even wait for an introduction! Common behavior one expects from a person raised in the Colonies, I suppose."

He pulled his gaze back from where it had danced along behind Miss Shaw. "We don't refer to them as the Colonies any longer, Eleanor."

Lady Chapman-Holmes gathered four centuries of exceptional breeding and stared down her nose at him, a mere viscount, number five. "As if I wouldn't know that woman, my lord. Francine Shaw, daughter of Archibald Shaw, the American investor. He's in London to talk railroads and marriage of his only child to the highest title he can purchase. Rumor is, he's drawing up agreements with Baron Hillsdale this very minute. You know Hillsdale's financial situation is abysmal, his father and brothers wastrels. She's been thrust into every event this season that would have her." She hummed, a grating sound that made him wish he'd never met her. Made him wish he could blow out a candle and ask for a different life.

"The Duchess Society sent her. I see. Your friendship with Hildegard Templeton... no, now it's Streeter. Dear God, she *married* that smuggler. She'd rather draw up those agreements with a viscount, wouldn't she? A smart business move on her part. But she is a shrewd woman."

Chance swallowed hard, stunned to his core. He'd rarely allowed himself to be played for a fool. That his childhood friend would do this to him—and Miss Shaw, with her innocent smiles and winsome nature —brought an ache to his heart he hadn't felt since his father turned his back on him years ago for refusing to give up his plan to manage a business *and* a viscountcy.

Why would the Duchess Society propel Miss Shaw across his path if it was anything *but* a trap?

Nevertheless, he realized his situation.

And Miss Shaw's. And Katherine's.

So, the lie came easily.

"I know who she is. There wasn't time to secure a proper governess, and Miss Shaw is a personal friend of Mrs. Streeter's who has experience with children, which I obviously do not. It's only until the new year. Her companion is in residence as well. Hildy and Tobias are on the way for the holiday. If you recall, they have a residence not a twenty-minute ride away. Nothing inappropriate in the event you thought to share this news. With Miss Shaw's expected marriage to Hillsdale, an untruth could be damaging." Chance crossed to the front door and yanked it open, his patience depleted. *Christ*, he was glad her carriage was waiting on the drive. "It's for the child, Eleanor. Her happiness as she settles into a new life is of utmost importance to me, believe it or not. If you make this afternoon anything else"—he bared his teeth, taking his anger out on her—"I'll consider it a personal affront. Do we understand each other?"

Lady Chapman-Holmes stalked past him, tying her bonnet string with trembling fingers. "I honestly don't know what I saw in you, Remington. You're as arrogant and thoughtless as they say."

"Likewise," Chance murmured dispassionately and shut the door behind her with a click.

A frigid gust swirled through the foyer, chilling him to the bone.

Leaning against the jamb, he knocked his head against the aged oak, betrayal enveloping him like a cloak.

Hildy Streeter and Francine Shaw were like all the rest.

Clawing their way to the top without consideration of who they trampled on the way up.

Chapter Four

Where Light is Shed on a Misunderstanding

S he couldn't sleep.

A thunderstorm had rolled in after sunset, snow turning to rain that pelted the windowpanes in steady, disturbing thumps. Franny had never liked storms. That night in Gerald's parlor, a downpour had hammered the sparkling new shingles of his home. A deluge that washed down her face as she stumbled from the house and into a waiting conveyance.

She didn't often conjure that incident, or tried not to, but when it rained like this, she couldn't help herself.

Clutching her portfolio to her chest, she searched for the library Mrs. Walker had shown her, a space that wasn't in quite as dismal a state as most of Rose Hill. Although in need of loving care, she was enchanted by the estate. Absolutely enchanted. Turrets and moats, portraits a hundred years old, room after room, stories this place would tell. Humming softly, she turned down a corridor, her footpads muted on the runner, then came to a swift halt.

Candlelight spilled like mist from an open door.

With a tightly drawn breath, she advanced. Despite the risk. There was likely only one person still awake.

But Franny could be honest with herself if no one else.

She was attracted to Lord Remington.

And had been from the moment she'd seen him crouched before that escritoire. The way he'd studied her over the breakfast table this morning, his eyes near the color of the vast sea she'd crossed to get to him, suggested he felt something as well, however slight.

However for men, attraction was rarely significant.

For women, it could be deadly.

She should know.

Franny paused in the doorway. It wasn't the library but rather a deserted chamber the viscount appeared to be using as his workshop. There were tools scattered atop a length of stained linen being used to protect the floors. Aged planks she wasn't sure needed protecting. Remington was on his haunches beside a partially constructed desk, working sandpaper over a rounded wooden block in his hand. Of most interest to her were the sketches he'd crudely tacked to the walls. Paintings had been removed to allow for this, dull squares stamped over faded wallpaper.

Knowing no way to make a delicate entrance, she wandered inside, crossing to the drawings. They were unrefined but workable diagrams, mostly of desks in some version of creation. She'd begun to see pieces scattered about the house that she assumed were his. The style bold and unmistakable, lodged somewhere between elegant and contemporary. For a moment, the sound of the rain striking the windowpanes was the only sound flowing between them.

"Miss Shaw," Remington said after a charged pause, his voice wavering slightly. It was then she noted the brandy bottle by his hip, the half-empty glass beside it. "You've found me. What a surprise."

She turned from her study of his schematics, unclear what he'd meant by the statement. Unclear about the heat behind his words. Gone was the profligate he presented to society. This man was a simmering cauldron, the ruthlessness he tried to hide shimmering like firelight around him. Perhaps he found it easier to sell the simpler version of himself.

She did that every day.

He gave the wood in his hand, what looked to be a table leg, a vigorous buff. "You've made changes during your short time in residence. Managing this house less like a governess and more like a woman who has managed her own. Decorations on the banisters and hearths. The parlors open to light, drapes beaten of dust, the scent of decay vanquished. You're friendly with the servants even."

"You mean I actually talk to them. I ask their names and about their families. You should try it. Everyone wants to be valued in this way."

"I wasn't raised to converse with domestics. Including governesses."

Franny settled back against the wall, clutching the portfolio to her chest. "You're angry with me."

Katherine was sleeping like a child who'd had a wonderful day. They'd decorated the house, brightening up what *was* a dismal residence. Had she done something untoward with the girl? Was it interrupting his meeting with the woman who was rumored to be his mistress?

She didn't want to contemplate the fury that had sizzled through her when Lady Chapman-Holmes's lips grazed his cheek. The seductive smile on her face speaking of ownership.

She'd wanted to do a very uncouth thing and sock the woman in her patrician nose.

Franny's desire to sketch the man was overruling common sense. And what little breeding she had.

Remington went to his knee to steady himself and, placing the wood aside, lifted the glass to his lips. "When you create a hinge for a gate leg, you have to round the teeth's edges so the hinge swings freely. But not too freely. You bullnose the corners. It's a negotiation with the wood." He sipped, his gaze finding hers across the distance. "Like life, a negotiation between what one wants and what one *gets*."

She drew a delicate breath, helplessly drinking him in. Competing shafts of light fought for his attention. The wall sconce above battling the candle at his side. His jaw was stubbled in grain so dark he looked like a pirate. His overlong hair tickled the crisp fold of his collar. His shirttail hit his hip; tattered trousers covered his long legs. Working clothes. Nothing he'd wear in the city. The muscles in his shoulders flexed as he stared at her staring at him, controlled displeasure.

"What have I done?" she finally asked, fine to be the one who buckled. Women were used to removing pride from the equation.

The viscount released a bitter huff, setting the glass to the floor with a clink. "You look at me like I'm cream, and you're a starving cat when you're engaged to Hillsdale? I begin to feel sorry for a reprehensible bloke I don't *like*."

Franny's exhalation left her lungs in a rush. So that was it. "I'm not engaged," she whispered. "The agreements are not signed."

"Are you sure about that, Miss Shaw?"

"I have to agree," she said, temper sparking her words. "I'm *not* engaged."

"You're also not a governess."

She swallowed, desperately wishing for a sip of brandy. "For the next two weeks, I am."

"Perhaps," he murmured and refilled his glass. Then he gazed at her through the curtain of inky hair falling across his brow.

Scooting the glass toward her, he nodded. *Have some.*

She wasn't going to deny the offer. Perhaps an English woman would, but an American one would not.

"Why did you do it?" Remington asked as she stepped closer, placing her portfolio on the floor and reaching for the glass. She had to go to her knees, putting them on equal, intimate footing. His scent, leather and something peppery, crept in to tease her senses. As if she needed more to snag her awareness. "To secure a destitute viscount? Couple notches higher than a baron, true. Although deception isn't typically the Duchess Society's style. Isn't Hildy's style, I should say. I've known her since we were in leading strings."

Franny was taking a sip when he made his claim. She coughed and scrubbed her wrist across her lips, the liquor burning a path down her throat. "Is that what you think? Hildegard Streeter had *nothing* to do with this. She was against the idea. Believe me." Franny would never forgive herself should her bit of whimsy damage his relationship with his friend. "I was there, in the corner of the room when you burst in. I volunteered for this."

He rocked back on his heels, giving her a thoroughly carnal review. She was dressed informally as well. *Too* informally. A sleeping gown covering every inch of her, but without the undergarments in place to contain her generous curves. Her hair braided and hanging over one shoulder, stray strands she could never control dusting her brow and cheek.

She looked a fright, she was sure.

He lifted the bottle to his lips, his gaze inscrutable. "Not possible. I would have noticed you."

"We've attended at least two of the same events in the past six months. Maybe three. Occupied the same parlor four days ago, and you had no idea I was there. I can prove it. Mrs. Streeter, she called you Chance."

He scowled, the arrogant cur not liking to lose even so much as a silly argument. "You must have been hiding. I would have seen you." He dragged the bottle across his bottom lip. Her belly clenched, a perilous signal to her growing attraction. *Oh*, he was beautiful in the light. "The enchantress has teeth, I see." With a wicked expression she couldn't decipher, he snatched her portfolio from the floor, untied the leather bind, and began flipping through the sheets. As if he had the right to.

"I saw you once before, at the earl's musicale," Franny blurted, breathless and panicked, aroused and bewildered. When he saw her sketches, the jig was up. "You were running your hand over an escritoire. I was on the veranda. I noticed you through the window. I wanted to sketch you, that's why I told Hildy I would come. Truthfully, I forced her hand." He continued to flip through the sheets, blinking rapidly, engrossed, while she babbled.

Her fascination was laid out in bold strokes her art instructor had stated were too extreme a representation for a female. There weren't many sketches of Viscount Remington yet, but the number was increasing. Rose Hill had proven to be inspirational, creatively. She could only thank the gods she'd not included anything risqué. Those were stuffed in the bottom of her portmanteau—derived from imagination only.

Although the trip up the staircase that first night, following along and watching his taut bottom flex had helped.

"You're quite gifted." He closed the portfolio and presented it to her with a sheepish, slated twist of his lips. He had a scar bleeding into the top one that she longed to press her tongue to. An image she'd never in her life envisioned.

Recognizing her absurd cravings, she grabbed her artwork and brought them back to her chest like a shield. "It's nothing. A hobby."

"It's attraction, Miss Shaw. We all feel it from time to time. Some more than others. It's rarely convenient. Although I've never seen it displayed in such an authoritative manner. Not personally. Tons of it on exhibit in museums, of course."

"I wanted to sketch you. That's all it was. All it *is*. It's what artists *do*."

Remington grinned, the bounder. Spreading his fingers wide across the floor for balance, he leaned in like a feral cat. *Damn and blast*, she wanted his hands on her. "If this an extreme case of infatuation, I find myself unduly flattered. Hell's teeth, you set up a novel deception simply to capture my face in charcoal. I believe this is the most any woman has ever done to establish contact with me. One not looking to be a viscountess, that is. There was a determined chit that shall go unnamed who climbed a tree to get into my bedchamber last year. *That* was noteworthy. I found I couldn't turn her away after such tremendous effort, in case you're wondering."

Franny rose to her feet with a growl, jealousy and embarrassment eating a hole in her belly. "It's *art*. I don't want any part of your blasted title! I truly don't want any part of *anyone's* title. Those are my father's dreams. I may have to fulfill them due to my own transgressions, which aren't a topic for discussion, but that's not your concern."

"Ah, yes, your young baron. Can I say, I'm more than happy to examine this dilemma of yours." He made a lazy X over his heart with his crossed fingers. "Our discussion will stay in my sparse parlor-cum-workshop, between friends. Or between governess and employer. We're still playing those roles, correct?"

"*What* dilemma?"

He was smirking, though he covered his mouth to hide it. She preferred this, even if it vexed her, to his anger. "Lust, sweetheart. Yours for me. Americans seem less concerned about hiding what they feel, which is unusual for an Englishman. We're not the most expressive of souls. And when we are, usually it's the man who has to break the proverbial ice." He flicked his hand between them, signaling there was an *us*. "This is bloody refreshing."

She spun on her heel, returning to his wall of sketches. "You're laughing at me, like the rest. The *ton* thinks I'm foolish and inappropriate. Vulgar. Why should you be any different? When it was my father who dragged me to this godforsaken country. My art is all that is mine alone."

She felt him move behind her, invading her space but without touching her. His brandy-laced breath slipped past her annoyance, melting her already fragile resistance. "I need you. Through Christmastide. Katherine likes you, and she was happy today. I saw it." His husky plea streaked in her ear, warming something inside her that had been cold for months. For years. Forever. "I'm not making fun of you. That isn't what this is. I'm an outsider in society myself. I always have been. Even if society doesn't realize it. They don't know the man, just the blessed title."

Franny lifted her hand to trace the imprecise marks of his drawing. Her fingers shook, and she pressed her knuckles to the wall to quell the reaction.

He reached to steady her, his arm aligning itself alongside hers as if he was showing her how to discharge a rifle. "It's a writing table." Taking her hand, he drew her fingertip along the parts as he rattled them off, his voice oozing the same liquid charisma she bet he used when he charmed someone out of their gown. "This is the pen tray. The leather skiver, twin tooled in gold. A brass keyhole lining to the frieze. Tapper legs, capped and footed with gilt capitols and mounts. It will be the most gorgeous piece in England when I'm done. I'll have one in Carlton House, you watch. Prinny, or the King now, I suppose I should say, will beg for it. The one love of my life, this work. Like your art, I understand. I *do*."

"I can do better representations for you," she murmured, struggling to lead him off course. He was half-foxed, and she was smitten. She knew enough from her past mistake to realize this was a lethal combination. Yet, she let herself stand there, mere inches separating their bodies, awareness as thick as London's fog encasing them in sensual heat. "I could try."

Remington straightened, his hand falling from hers as he stepped back. "They're my designs, each and every one. But my drawings aren't good. It's a problem. Nevertheless, when I've tried to describe what I *want* to an illustrator, it's been off. I can't find anyone who can capture my vision."

The challenge was there, the need to solve it undefined and reckless. To please him in this way. "What do I get in return if I do this for you? If I'm able to capture your vision on paper?" She turned to find his intent gaze focused on her, unwavering. Absurdly, she loved that he was intelligent *and* uncompromising. "Consider it repayment for misleading you, even if my intentions were genuine."

"There must be a trade." He tapped his chin in thought. "How about this? I'll sit for your sketches."

Her hand clenched around her portfolio. She struggled for a clever response when she wasn't a clever woman. Her witty retorts always arrived an hour too late.

His lips tilted, a small dent that could possibly be called a dimple pinging his cheek. That lank of hair jutting out, calling her hand to smooth it. "Can I ask about clothing, as much of the portraits I've seen feature men who are... how shall I delicately say this? Unclothed. I feel I should call you Franny if you're set to see me in the buff."

Her cheeks burned while lascivious images assaulted her mind. "Your normal attire"—she flicked her hand toward him, brow to toe —"will be adequate." Although she longed to know. If she asked him to disrobe, would he *do* it? "But you can call me Franny. I don't mind."

"Then you may call me Chance." He shrugged, humming beneath his breath. "I had a high fever as a babe, for days, but I survived. My mother felt it was a remarkable piece of luck as she'd lost a child to something similar. She called me her lucky chance. But she died before I truly got to know her." He frowned when he finished the explanation, as if he'd not considered what he was disclosing. Or to whom.

Hoping to break the intimate moment, Franny carefully removed one of his drawings from the wall. "Can I take this? I'd like to create a more detailed illustration. Anything is better than a blank page, as they say."

Remington stepped in, his gaze searching. First the sketch in her hand, then a lingering assessment starting at the hem of her sleeping gown and concluding just past her chest. After a charged moment where it seemed he was deciding what to do, he reached to tuck a strand of hair behind her ear. He dawdled, caressing her cheek. His blue eyes were shot through with flecks of gold, she noted at this distance, truly dazzling in the candlelight. His jaw muscle flexed as his lips pressed tight, his own ideas running loose.

Kiss me, she thought wildly.

With a muted sigh, he shook himself free, his gaze dropping to his drawing. "Add a finial here," he tapped the parchment. "And here. The legs need to be more elegant. More in line with the design of the desk-top. Not too delicate. See what you can come up with. As you said, it's easier to edit than create."

Then he crossed to the door, and she had the feeling she was chasing a fox from his lair. He paused in the threshold, candlelight shining in his eyes. "Thank you for agreeing to this, for any reason you agreed. I want Katherine to be happy, and somehow, I'm going to find a way to make sure that happens."

Then he was gone.

And all she could think was, *I want him back.*

⁓

He'd almost kissed her.

In fact, Chance had wanted many things in that moment.

It stunned him to realize who his phony governess was. Francine Shaw. Heiress to a mad American fortune. One of the so-called title-chasers flooding the city. Now that it had been pointed out to him, he recalled reading about her in the *Gazette's* gossip column.

Nothing the author had stated matched the woman, however.

She was an intriguing mix of daring and naivete. Embarrassment and hunger crossing her face in swift intervals. Her expression *begging* him to kiss her. The look of unconcealed longing sending an aroused rush through him.

What would it be like to seduce someone who wanted you but didn't *want* to want you?

Chance knew what a melting glance meant. The skip in breathing, a fierce pulse tapping at the base of a woman's neck. Francine Shaw was lovely in an understated, absolutely compelling manner. Gorgeous eyes near the color of the calla lilies that bloomed outside his Mayfair bedchamber in spring. A mix of hazel and gold. Too, her bloody hair was indescribable.

What he would pay to see *that* glory spread across his sheets.

And her body. A goddess in conspicuously unattractive clothing. He'd about choked when she strolled into the library, every curve she possessed on display in that hideous dressing gown.

Incredibly, Chance questioned if he ought to use his title as a bargaining chip. Because his intriguing governess was far too interesting a package for that fop Hillsdale.

After all, she'd done the near impossible.

She'd ignited his senses for the first time in *ages*. Maybe it was the scent of lilacs and a hint of lemon that drifted like snowflakes around her. Or her accent, flat as the moors, but charming in its unfussiness. He'd pay a thousand pounds to hear her whisper in his ear as she came around him. Thinking this at an inopportune time, he'd been forced to stalk from the room like a man possessed before she noticed his cock threatening to bust his bone buttons.

How had he missed her at the Earl of Devlin's musicale?

Odd, as he'd never been attracted to an *American* before.

It was too bad really. Timing and circumstance not meeting in the middle. Her needing a title and him needing blunt to keep the viscountcy afloat. But he'd promised himself he'd never marry without love after growing up in a home without it. Head and heart needed to be in alignment for him to promise his future to anyone.

The lonely little boy he'd been demanded it.

Sighing, he gazed across the lawn from his perch on the veranda wall, his breath fogging the air, his fingers frozen from the chill. The rain had stopped a half hour ago, leaving a damp, leaden mist to color the world a snowy white. He was coming to quite appreciate Derbyshire. For all the reasons his father had hated it. It was remote. Untamed. The air crisp and clean. The land stretching to the horizon calling to him in a possessive, elemental way. *His* land. Custody he'd never felt about anything outside his furniture.

He'd told Francine Shaw about his nickname. He'd talked about his mother, the only person who had shown him love that he could recall.

Something he never, ever did.

The story of his family wasn't an uplifting tale, and he rarely found the need to share it.

Her serene presence, the mix of goodness and heat shimmering in her eyes, unlocked something in him. And the other...

Her illustrations had aroused him more than he'd thought a mere sketch could. Sent a ragged claw of need straight through him. They'd been drawings in various phases of completion. Mostly of his face. His hands. He lifted one and stared at it, spread his fingers, wondering what she saw that he didn't.

The man in those sketches had a regal, confident bearing—when Chance was uncertain. About life and his place in it. His ruse was nearly as great as hers. He played the charming viscount while struggling to locate the person beneath. A burden deposited on his shoulders at the ripe age of nineteen. When he'd had another passion altogether.

He worried over his relief when he'd realized Francine Shaw hadn't played him for a fool. She had her own troubles. Transgressions, she'd called them. Who knew what bit of mischief had had her running to England. Anyway, what did he care if his temporary governess was after his title? Like a thousand and one inane chits before her.

But he did care.

He blew a frosty breath into the sky, wishing for another glass of brandy.

This realization was disconcerting indeed.

Chapter Five

Where a Forlorn Viscount Opens His Heart. A Little.

K at had been staring at him for the past ten minutes from her spot on the faded Aubusson. She had a ragdoll of unknown origin clutched in her fist. She'd wandered in with a biscuit and the toy, settling herself on the floor without a word.

Strangely, he found the sound of her frayed breathing comforting. She had a stuffy nose from yesterday's activities in the snow, but he figured the fun had been worth it.

Chance placed the quill aside and leaned back in his chair. He was in his study, a chamber that had housed the resident viscount for generations. Although, he'd changed enough about the room to drive out the ghost of his father. Mostly. Starting with a desk of his own design. New curtains. Wallpaper. The little he could afford had gone into this space to help eradicate the memories.

Now, he would channel his meager funds into the nursery. The girl needed a better one than she currently had. Here and in London. He was set to sell two desks next week, which would provide blunt through the summer. He hoped. Tobias Streeter had offered a loan if he fell short, but he was hesitant to take an offer that indebted him to anyone.

"You're a viscount," Kat murmured while he sat there formulating what he could possibly say to start a conversation with a child. "Is that higher than a king? The last uncle I stayed with was the second son of a baron. He was ancient and smelled like peas. But he gave me gumdrops on occasion."

Chance rolled his lips in to hold back his laughter. "Much lower than a king. And I'm not your uncle. I'm your cousin through my mother's side of the family. *Your* mother was her second cousin, I believe. That would make me your third."

Kat gave an inelegant shrug, smoothing her hand down the doll's snarled ginger yarn hair. "I don't remember her."

Chance traced his finger over a blemish in the wood that he particularly loved. He'd chosen this piece for the desktop because of the mark. He'd always thought beauty lay in imperfection. "I don't remember mine very well, either."

Kat glanced up at this, seemingly startled to find they had anything in common. "You don't?"

Chance shook his head, wondering at speaking twice in two days of a woman he rarely recalled except in his dreams. It was being here, at Rose Hill. Where he'd lived with his mother until her death. Then at the tender age of five, he'd been shipped to the city to reside with a father who clearly hadn't wanted children. "She was lovely. I have her eyes and not much else. She was kind. Patient. She liked gardening and spent much of her time in the conservatory. Which is now in shambles."

Kat thought hard about this, twisting her doll's braid around her finger. "Can I be the next viscount? I can fix it up."

Chance's heart gave a hard thump. "That will go to my son. The eldest. Even if I have a daughter first. But you will be their older sister."

She sighed longingly. "No girls as viscount. That's not fair."

Chance gave his teacup a spin. "No, it isn't."

"Franny says women must work twice as hard in this world to make up for the inaccuracies."

He laughed, charmed. "Inequities."

Kat rose, the doll dangling from her fingers. She crossed to the desk and with confidence born of youth, circled his diagram into view. Her nose wrinkled with her frown. "Your desk looks crooked. One leg is shorter than the other. Franny is a much better artist. Maybe you should ask her."

"Actually, she's working on a drawing for me. Perhaps two even."

Kat's bright green eyes flicked to his. She chewed on her lip, debating, then blurted out, "She said you sent for gifts. For Christmastide. For me."

He recovered quickly. It was not the first time a woman had stunned him with the notion that he'd overlooked a special occasion. "I think rather than tell you, I'll let it be a surprise. Aren't surprises better?" he asked, wondering what he could find in the village at short notice.

Kat grinned and shifted from foot to foot. "I like surprises."

He was reaching before he had time to ponder the decision. His hand covered hers. It was small, her skin warm and... quite perfect. She turned, linking her fingers with his.

He hadn't held hands with anyone since his mother's passing.

A foreign emotion traveled through him, settling firmly in his chest.

Of course, his errant governess arrived to find man and child beaming at each other across a desk, unspoken promises floating between them.

Franny cleared her throat, hesitating in the doorway.

Light from the sconces washed over her, igniting sparks in her glorious hair and across her freckled cheeks. She had an ink smear on the sleeve of another atrocious gown. He'd never known a woman in more desperate need of a modiste. Hideous clothing, however, couldn't hide her beauty. Too, he liked that she didn't seem to care for such things as gowns and fripperies. A folio was clutched in her hand and the expression on her face—tentative excitement—led him to believe she'd come with sketches to share.

Her companion stepped behind her. Ada's shrewd gaze instantly found Chance's, her scowl growing. The woman was no fool and recognized his attraction. Probably because it sat out there like a lazy cat snoozing in the sun. Then she looked to Franny, recognizing her charge faced the same dilemma. Sighing, she jabbed Franny in the side with a murmured oath.

"Excuse us," Franny said and stumbled into the room. "Ada is going to take Kat down for her lunch. Then a nap."

Kat groaned and wiggled her hand from his. He missed the feeling of contentment immediately. "I don't want to. We're having fun."

Chance felt a smile lift his lips. *Fun?* Perhaps this child-rearing business was easier than he'd thought. Straightforward conversation. Touches. Promises of gifts. Was that all there was to it? It wasn't much different a set-up than with his mistresses. Young or old, women were women.

Franny's soft snicker snapped him out of his musing. Her golden eyes fixed on him; her lips parted in amusement. Somehow, she knew what he was thinking. This insight brought comfort and panic. He'd gotten used to feeling alone in a ballroom. Isolated in a city packed with distractions. Lonely in a bed with rumpled sheets, the warm body of someone he didn't love lying beside him.

To have Francine Shaw see him was exhilarating and *terrifying*.

"Go on," he urged when he was sure his voice wasn't going to shake, shooing Kat from the room. "Young ladies need their beauty sleep. We'll talk more at dinner. You can tell me about the decorations you've placed all over the house."

Groaning, she clutched the threadbare ragdoll to her chest and trudged across the room. Ada gave him a piercing glare—*look but don't touch*—then escorted Kat from the room. He vowed then and there that the girl would have a new doll for Christmas.

Franny watched them go before turning to him.

Nervous. She was definitely nervous. Deciding to take pity on them both, Chance tossed her a lifeline. When he'd never felt like seducing someone more—or acting on the impulse less. "I've heard I'm to provide gifts for Christmas. I'm glad Kat informed me before it was too late."

Instead of flushing with mortification, Franny laughed, and stepped into the room. "They're arriving tomorrow. I know you have enough to worry over." She flicked her hand around the space, a benevolent gesture meant to encompass his wealth of responsibilities. "This is part and parcel of what I agreed to. Take care of the child."

"Responsibilities as in, low on funds to purchase gifts. My dire situation is fodder for gossip, I realize. Most of the mamas throwing their daughters my way have introduced the topic of finances first, before beauty or skill with the pianoforte. My father wasn't an able fiscal manager. In fact, he was a profligate gambler, unconcerned with the inconvenience he was leaving me to handle. Estates and no funds. A brother in need of guidance. For myself, I don't care so much, I make enough to survive with the furniture, but the staff, the tenants..."

He dragged his hand through his hair, his breath shortening as it did when he thought of the lives attached to the viscountcy's payroll. When he thought of Arthur. His brother was fragile in ways he'd never been. "Some servants have worked on the estates, three including the townhouse in Mayfair, for most of their lives."

Her chagrin arrived, flushing her cheeks a rosy hue. Yet she didn't deny the assertion. He was destitute, and everyone in London knew it.

Chance sprawled in his chair, stacking his hands over his belly. Her gaze followed the movement, lingering on his chest, then rising to his face. Her eyes were a golden explosion, heaps of emotion contained in their fiery depths. He had to work to hear her soft exhalation. *Christ*, he wanted that sound skating across his skin while he sank inside her. More than he wanted his next breath. Indeed, his attraction was astonishing. He could see no way he'd been in the same room with her and not *felt* it. He must have confused the vibration for something else, not knowing what he was feeling.

He swallowed hard, his throat dry. What had they been discussing?

"Presents," she murmured. Again, knowing where his mind had gone.

"Is a doll arriving in the shipment?"

She nodded. "Of course. What little girl doesn't want a new doll? And sweets, as the English call them, when we simply say candy. Books. Boots. A dress."

"You're the most efficient member of my staff, Miss Shaw. Thank you. The last thing I want to do is disappoint her." He shrugged, discomfited. Scrubbed the back of his neck with his hand. "Although I don't know how to please her, either. My brother is the only person I've tried to accommodate, and that hasn't worked out so well."

Franny took three steps until her hip hit the edge of his desk.

Because she'd done the same without concealing it, Chance let his gaze travel the length of her. Following Ada's unspoken advice, he wouldn't touch, but he would *look* all he pleased. Trap visions of her lush curves in his mind, the swell of her breast pressing against her bodice, and use them. Later, in his massive medieval bed. Where he'd stroke himself to completion while fantasizing of the sweetly guileless American who had stumbled into his life.

"Is this the way you look at every woman?" she asked breathlessly. "If it is, I understand."

He wrenched forward in his chair, his hands going to the desk to brace himself. "Excuse me?"

She leaned in, palming the wood as he had, her hands settling on each side of his. Her gown dipped at the neck, allowing a slender view of the rounded slopes of her breasts. He dragged his gaze to hers with extreme effort while his cock hardened beneath buckskin. His fingertips tingled, his body tensing in anticipation. "I understand why half of London is desperate to get to you. Climbing inside second-story windows for even one moment basking in the intensity of your regard. I've heard of a man undressing you with his eyes, but I've never experienced it." She licked her lips, and he felt his breath sucked from his lungs. "Until now. It's quite... extraordinary."

Touch her, Chance, round this desk and touch her.

Seduce her, you're bloody good at it.

But he sat, immobile, aroused beyond measure. Dazed. A thousand responses flowing through his mind, not one worthy of her. Glowing with the rush of finding a treasure no one in England had discovered, he stumbled into the moment, unsure. Franny Shaw was the most delightful piece he'd ever encountered. She actually said what she meant. She was honest. Beautiful. Kind. Giving. Unique.

And... *no. One. Knew.*

There had to be something wrong with her. There *must* be something wrong with her. No chit could be this perfect.

The colossal difference in their upbringing unfurled like a carpet between them as they stared, lost to the sensual fog enveloping them. She'd not been taught that one didn't discuss seduction in such a forthright manner. One didn't admit attraction unless the reputations involved were irretrievably tainted, and so far, only *his* was.

She hadn't been taught that you hid everything from everyone to protect yourself. He didn't have enough courage to display himself thusly.

"I think you'd better go," he whispered, his voice ragged. If she continued to gaze at him like this, her desire his for the taking, he was going to drag her to the door, lock it, and shove her against it. He *loved* tupping standing up.

And he would make sure she left unable to ever, *ever* forget him.

"I have sketches of the desk. Two versions. As you requested, I placed the—"

"Leave them," he growled and grabbed the folio from her hand. "I thank you in advance. I desperately need assistance. I do. However, either you're leaving this room right now, or I'm coming around the desk to kiss the blessed breath from you. Push you against the wall and show you what the heat of my regard *really* feels like. My desire to erase every thought from your mind is blindingly compelling. Draw the air from your lungs into mine. Send you into a molten puddle at my feet, one I'll happily follow. It's your choice, of course. Completely. Your. Choice. But I'm shaky. And close to making it for you."

She hesitated, damn her. Lifted her hand to her lips and gave them the lightest caress. His body lit as he scrubbed his hand across his own. Raw *want* pierced him, weakening his resolve to do the right blasted thing for once.

He was rising, done, ready to test this attraction between them when she released a quivering sigh he would take to his grave, turned, and fled through the open doorway.

Leaving a provoked viscount to sift through the remnants of his yearning.

Chapter Six

The village seamstress jabbed her with a needle without Franny feeling a thing. Which was her own fault. She'd never been able to stand still during fittings with her modiste, which could account for her gown's shortcomings.

This fidgeting, however, was due to Viscount Remington.

Since the incident in his study, she'd been walking around in a fever dream. Her skin sensitized to the slightest caress of muslin or lace. Her breath teasing lips that were bruised from her touch and sadly, *only* her touch.

Damn and blast, she thought hotly. He'd taken something from her without her even realizing she was relinquishing it. And he hadn't even let her sketch him as he'd promised.

Although, he'd occupied her dreams for two nights, his body covering hers, the fantasy bleeding into a mix of heat and sensual urgency, her frustration staggering when she woke to an empty bed and cool sheets.

Strangely enough, they were working together. Or working *apart* might be the better way to describe it.

They were passing her sketches back and forth, in ways that limited the chance they'd find themselves alone in the same room again. She'd gotten used to deciphering his scribbled modifications in the margins, the sheets left during the night on a desk she'd appropriated in a library that regrettably contained few books. She returned the revised drafts to his workshop each morning.

They were getting close to the design of the desk he wanted in Carlton House. Theirs was a partnership unlike any she'd envisaged she would have.

Ada knew something had happened between them. Franny couldn't get much past her. Consequently, her companion had not let Franny out of her sight.

Until the Duchess Society stepped back into the picture.

Hildy Streeter had stopped by the evening prior to check on a situation she'd not agreed to, and upon seeing the gown Franny had selected to wear to Lord Grimley's ball, quickly located a seamstress who could modify one of hers. She was taller than Franny, her curves less plentiful, but with a skilled craftsman, it would do. Georgiana Munro, the Duchess of Markham, Hildy's partner in the Duchess Society, had also arrived and was currently trying to arrange Franny's hair into something resembling a chignon. Ada wasn't skilled, and Remington had no maid on staff who was.

"I shouldn't be going." Franny stilled lest the needle make another strike, but her toe tapped a furious rhythm on the carpet. "Lord Grimley and I haven't been introduced. My father hasn't done business with him even. No one is expecting me. I'm an American version of a wallflower. Worse. I promise you that I add nothing to the event."

Hildy seethed in ladylike decorum from her spot on the threadbare settee jammed in the corner of Franny's bedchamber. The hulking furniture did not fit the space. Like most of the rooms at Rose Hill, this one was a jumble of masculine embellishment and blatant neglect. "Being recognized by Lady Chapman-Holmes of all people made the decision, Miss Shaw. *Everyone* in Derbyshire is expecting you. Lord Remington stated publicly that I knew about this governess arrangement, almost as if I was your chaperone. So, you'll accompany me and prove it. There are rules to uphold. The baron agreed to the latest set of contracts, and we've forwarded them to your father's local solicitor. Hillsdale was unsettled by the rumor of you being in the residence of a notorious rake, even if properly accompanied, so he arranged for transport he cannot afford, and he'll also be in attendance."

"Can't blame him, considering the viscount's horrid reputation," the duchess mumbled around the hair clip jammed between her teeth. "Dogs like to fight over their bones, don't they? Maybe Remington assuming care of a child will polish off a few of his rough edges. It won't make the hungry mamas harass him any less, that's certain, but perhaps he'll forgo a mistress for a bit. That would help."

"Bother," Franny whispered, her heart giving a jarring thud. The thought of Chance Allerton and his sizzling glances, and Baron Hillsdale and his tepid ones, occupying the same space made her want to crawl beneath her ratty counterpane and hide until spring. While the thought of the viscount's many mistresses made her want to break something.

"Have you talked to him?" This question was thrown over Franny's head by the duchess—who had asked to be called Georgie—to her partner in crime, Hildy. They'd held multiple hushed conversations while she stood there fuming. "Close friends, aren't you?"

"Chance? We're distant cousins, actually." Hildy smoothed her hand over her gently rounded stomach with a clever smile. She was expecting in a few months, and her excitement was surpassed only by her husband's. All of London was commenting on Tobias Streeter's transformation from rookery brawler to lovesick husband. "Oh, he's avoiding me."

The women looked to her as if Franny knew the reason behind this.

Franny's lips parted, a terse exhalation slipping free. "He's working." And riding his midnight-black bay across the frozen landscape each morning like he was fleeing from something. Or someone. "A new desk design. It's actually quite lovely. Gorgeous finials and these tapered, very elegant legs. Rosewood, I think he said he's going to use. I—" Halting, she realized she'd said too much. In a tone that spoke of familiarity well above a governess's lot.

"Oh, dear," Georgie murmured, giving a lock of Franny's hair a yank. "I was afraid of this."

While Hildy simply watched, waiting. Patient but expectant. She was going to make a magnificent mother if she used these dead stares on her children when they'd done something wrong. It was worse than a ruler across the knuckles, which her father had employed many times.

"I'm helping him," Franny finally said. Then stronger. "He doesn't have an artist who understands his vision."

"His vision," Hildy whispered into the hand she'd bought to her lips. "His *vision*. I'm going to kill him. How about *that* for a vision, Chance Allerton?"

Franny gave the seamstress, Mrs. Smithe, who was also a midwife in the village, a chagrined grimace. "Perhaps it's good enough? I like the fit." She wasn't going to mention that Lord Remington had begun tacking her sketches up alongside his own on his workshop wall.

Mrs. Smithe sucked her cheek between her teeth, running her hand over the altered waist of a gown that was the loveliest Franny had ever worn. She'd never cared much about clothing or had anyone special to dress for. "If you don't eat a thing this evening, not so much as one biscuit, it might work. I wouldn't exhale too hard, either. Dancing is questionable. You are slightly more endowed"—she wagged her hands to describe a fuller figure, then nodded to Hildy—"than the missus. Keep a shawl handy just in case you split a seam."

Franny's cheeks flushed. She was *healthy*, according to Ada, who had a vile, defensive hatred of slender figures. "Thank you for the advice. I appreciate your prompt assistance."

Mrs. Smithe whistled and gathered up her basket of materials, stabbing needles in the velvet cushion strapped to her wrist. Crimson thread matching Franny's gown dangled from her sleeve and her bodice. "Dear heart, you paid me London wages for Derbyshire work. I'm not even the best seamstress in the village. But it'll do. And so will I. My stitches are straight and strong, don't you worry. But don't go and cough, not even once."

Georgie covered a burst of laughter with the hairbrush and escorted Mrs. Smithe into the hallway.

Once they were alone, Franny rounded on Hildy. "There's no reason to hurt him. I'm helping Lord Remington, true, but we're barely speaking if that makes you feel better. It's the most distant business relationship imaginable. He's not coming to dinner or breakfast while Kat and I are there."

Her hand going to her lower back, Hildy stretched with a muted groan, her gaze taking no prisoners. Franny could see how she'd captured the most cunning man in London. She was a fierce competitor. "He's avoiding me, avoiding you. Why is that, do you think?"

Knowing exactly why that was, Franny decided it was a perfect time to test the gown's seams, circling the room, trailing her fingers across dusty shelves, making a mental note to have someone clean the room. This house would take a year of hard labor to get in order. With a sinking heart, she realized Remington would soon marry, and it would be his viscountess making sure that happened.

"My husband did something similar after we kissed the first time. He made quite a show of running, Miss Shaw. I know what men trying to escape a realization look like."

Franny did a slow rotation on the balls of her feet. "We didn't kiss." She hadn't kissed anyone since that disaster in Philadelphia. She'd wanted to kiss Lord Remington, of course. What woman wouldn't? He was the most handsome man in England. Tall, dark, and...

Hildy snorted, an inelegant sound from an elegant woman. "You should see the dreamy expression on your face. Whatever happened was enough to have the viscount making a respectful fool of himself. When I told him you were off-limits. About to be married to Hillsdale. The man is a menace. A bounder. A scoundrel. I presented a challenge he can't deny. Unless..." Hildy sat up, her feet hitting the floor with a *thump*. "You want to marry Hillsdale, don't you?"

Franny gave a half-hearted shrug. "Truthfully, I don't want to marry anyone. If not for my father and his threats, I'd live my life as a sketching spinster. But I want freedom, financial and personal, and it seems marriage is my only way to get it. I'm purchasing a husband if I may be bold, so I have control I wouldn't otherwise have." She picked up a vase with a chipped edge and ran her thumb over the imperfection. She'd always thought imperfections made a piece. She didn't want to tell Hildy about the scandal that had brought her here. It didn't really matter except in the depths of her heart. "Look at the vexed expression on *your* face. You believe in love. Matchmakers often do. It's not surprising. But it's not reality, either. I've never known anyone to marry for anything but business. My parents included. My mother's dowry backed his first company. He didn't come from money, believe it or not. Baron Hillsdale's children won't have a storied birthright, but they won't be destitute, either."

"We're not matchmakers, but I believe in love. I'm in the midst of living it. I want what I have with Tobias for every woman who crosses the Duchess Society's threshold. Every woman in England. There's no greater joy than marrying the *one* person you can't live without. I would have gone anywhere with Toby, marriage or no. Followed him to the ends of the earth and back. He had me from the first moment, the first word. I can't explain it. I only know it's what I felt." She smiled softly, her hand settling on her stomach in a protective gesture. "What I *feel*. I also understand this isn't practical for most."

Franny placed the vase back on the shelf, turning the chipped side to the front. "There's truly no reason to delay. My father and I agree this is the best choice for me." Acting on an infatuation with the most infamous rake in London wasn't a wager she could safely make.

But she would have liked a kiss.

She glanced over her shoulder, a sense of urgency driving her toward something. "So, you'll continue to help me? Until we have the papers signed?"

Hildy slumped to the settee, grooves of exhaustion streaking from the corners of her eyes. "Of course. That's what I was hired to do, but I won't be happy about it."

I won't either, Franny thought woefully.

Chapter Seven

Where a Forlorn Viscount Ponders the Rules of Attraction

Chance hated balls. They made him feel like he was standing outside his body, watching the proceedings from an ambiguous vantage point. As if his clothing was two sizes too small or his skin covered in hives.

As if he was playing a role and doing a bloody pitiable job of it.

Although this event was smaller than most, sold as a winter celebration in case the melted snow mucked across the marble floor, the pine branches tacked to every ready surface, it wasn't a clear reminder of the season.

Winter simply meant it was too frigid to open the veranda doors to invite even the suggestion of fresh air. So here he stood, the scent of sweat mixing unpleasantly with lemon verbena and pine. Every starving mama in the room giving him a jaundiced eye because he'd yet to sign so much as one dance card. He dragged the toe of his Wellington, not boots meant for dancing, mind you, through a layer of chalk on the floor. In use so one didn't go careening across marble, landing on one's bum. An occurrence which would have made the festivities a bit more interesting at least.

"You're going to have to dance with someone, mate. Your role as a nobleman, innit? Give the unattached ladies some hope for the future? Their mother's stares are starting to torch my skin," Xander Macauley said, shoving a beverage that Chance prayed was stronger than champagne in his hand. "Glad they don't want anything to do with me."

Macauley was Tobias Streeter's partner, London's finest smuggler since Streeter had stepped down when he'd gotten married and started a family. Both men had grown up in the slums and now ruled parts of the city most had never visited or *wanted* to visit. Macauley owned a shipping company, a distillery, and half a dozen other incredibly profitable ventures. Rumor was, a gaming hell was next. Chance's partnership with Streeter, Macauley & Company had earned him enough blunt to keep from being so desperate he would have signed every dance card in the building during the first ten minutes of his arrival.

And as friends, they'd protected his identity. No one in the *ton* knew Washburn Furnishings was his. Washburn had been his mother's maiden name.

Although he couldn't avoid marriage to some dazzlingly wealthy blue-blooded chit forever. Even with his love promise. Only this morning, he'd found a rather substantial leak in the roof at Rose Hill. In a back parlor. One that could potentially bleed him dry to repair. His chest ached when he thought about the care the estate needed. A life that now included a little girl.

Lifting his gaze to the gilt-edged ceiling, Chance tossed back half the drink—scotch, thank God—in one punch.

"There you go, Remington, grease the wheels for the night you're set to have. No need for sobriety for this." Macauley leaned his broad shoulder on the column Chance had chosen to hide behind, elegance in nonchalant repose.

Chance grimaced and finished off the scotch, welcoming the path it burned down his throat. What did Macauley know about it? He had enough blunt to fund a country's takeover and absolutely no expectation that he'd marry anyone above an opera singer or possibly an actress. He could fall in love with his *mistress* and make it come out all right. As long as he didn't try to climb higher, he was fine.

"Quit frowning, mate. Your night has just gotten a lot more interesting."

Chance swiveled to face the ballroom, his gaze sweeping the revolving couples, then climbing the spiral staircase at the opposite end of the hall. He blinked, momentarily blinded by a thousand candles' glow. Awareness shot down his spine before he recognized her, landing regrettably in his nether region. A response he struggled to hide with an arm dropped low.

His cock never played fair. Not once in his life.

This is what he'd feared but hadn't needed to see. Her beauty on display. Franny Shaw after someone with knowledge of English fashion got their hands on her. Her hair, for once contained in a stylish coiffure, sparking in the light until it glowed. And the gown. Layer upon layer of crimson silk leaving absolutely *nothing* to the imagination. She looked like she'd been sewn into the bloody thing. He nearly groaned as his gaze ate her up, feet to brow and back again. Like a gift he yearned to unwrap with his *teeth*.

Hildy had arranged this. Dangling the chit before him when she *knew*—oh, he wasn't fooling anyone—he was attracted. Frankly, his pulse started throbbing when she entered a room. He exhaled sharply, trying to ignore the way her breasts shifted as she descended the stairs into the ballroom.

She had the most gorgeous figure he'd ever set eyes on.

And unlike the others, her mind and heart were quite remarkable, too.

Macauley grinned, jamming his elbow into Chance's ribs. "*Ah*, the look on your face might make this dull-as-shite country jaunt noteworthy, as your posh set likes to say. Noteworthy as hell. I'm suddenly glad I accepted Streeter's offer. Your governess is a far sight prettier than I'd heard." He whistled softly between his teeth. "That is one delectable piece. Without the silly English prattle to deal with."

Chance slammed his glass on the tray of a passing footman, causing the servant to balance it with both hands before it tumbled to the floor. "Stay away, understood? She isn't like the ones you keep."

Macauley chuckled but there was a brutal edge racing beneath it. "She's not like the ones you keep, either."

Unfortunately, this was true.

"Hold up," Macauley whispered and took hold of his arm. He nodded to the bloke elbowing his way through the crowd to get to her. "Her betrothed, am I right? Even I occasionally take a look at the gossip rags. You don't need to get there panting like a horse out of the gate."

Chance yanked his arm free as Hillsdale arrived at the bottom of the staircase—just as Franny was set to officially enter the madness. He could have sworn the baron glanced back with a triumphant smirk. "They haven't signed any agreements."

"Hold on, I need another drink if we're discussing marital contracts," Macauley groused, going in search while Chance stood there, tucked behind a column, pondering the sentiment that had his belly tied in a quivering knot.

Franny went through the motions; he'd give her that. Smiled at the baron. Made a feminine show of offering her dance card, which Hillsdale signed twice with a flourish. When everyone knew two signified intent. She took a glass of champagne and sipped carefully. Only Chance noted her stiff posture, overly precise. The uncomfortable stretch of her lower back. The charcoal stain on the tip of her glove. The wrinkle on her bodice.

No one in this bloody country had any idea she was *real* beneath the posturing.

The most unique woman in the room.

Somehow, it had settled in his mind that Hillsdale was marrying her for her money. And he'd accepted this. But when the baron gazed down her bodice, his face getting the look only an aroused man's did, Chance realized he was entering virgin territory.

He'd never been jealous of any woman. Not once, ever.

"Drink this," Macauley muttered and bounced a tumbler off Chance's clenched fist. "We're not brawling tonight, at least until his babe is born. Streeter made me promise. No more. He'll be here any second with a wife glued to his side, a chit who has little tolerance for our antics. That gives us six months or so to exercise our wisdom.

Hildy told me I had it in me to be better if I'd only try. Fetching simple, innit? But for me, nothing about women seems simple."

Chance took the glass and sipped, his gaze fastened on Miss Shaw, who had begun to waltz with the baron. Her step was sure, almost athletic, impressive for a girl he imagined hadn't grown up waltzing. Chance had learned from a pitiless French instructor when he was twelve, at his father's command.

It had been harrowing and unpleasant, like much of his childhood.

Finally, on a swift turn, Franny caught his gaze. Her cheeks were rosy from exertion, but the bloom on them increased when she looked at him. Her silky smile reminded him of a gold- and-pink dusted dawn, brightening everything it touched. A buoyant sense of wonder stole through him. It was seconds that they stared, no more, but it was enough to confirm that Chance wasn't the only entranced soul.

Somehow, this knowledge bound him to her with invisible threads of need.

It was easy, *so* easy, to imagine what he'd do to her if given the opportunity. He'd start by unfastening the buttons of her bodice. Sliding the silken bundle from her shoulders to pile at her feet. Chemise ties loosened. Lace swept aside. Breasts straining for attention. Nipples pebbling as he tugged them between his lips. He wanted to mark her, change her. Turn them inside out. Situate himself between her thighs and stay there until she screamed.

He was *very* good at persuading without saying a word.

And he wanted to persuade Francine Shaw more than any woman of his acquaintance.

Without tearing his gaze from her, he asked, "Macauley, can you get something here by Christmas?"

"Three days until the day, mate. Gonna cost you. But I control half of the shipping channels in London, so anything can be bought. And I do mean damn near anything." He slipped a cheroot from his waistcoat pocket and wiggled it between his lips. "As your friend, because blunt is tight, I suppose it's gonna cost *me*. For the girl, I'm guessing? I can secure any toy you wish to put your hands on."

Chance rubbed the glass back and forth across his lips. He could ask Macauley for this favor when he wouldn't ask Tobias Streeter.

Because Hildy's husband was in love and at the stage where he wanted everyone *else* to be. Macauley didn't believe in love. In fact, he often compared the emotion to an infection. He'd never suspect Chance was doing anything aside from trying to get into a chit's drawers. "Her presents are hidden at the bottom of my wardrobe. Doll, new clothes, sweets. Even a puzzle of a duck in a lake or some such. She's swimming in gifts. What I need is for the governess."

Macauley grunted, the unlit cheroot bobbing between his lips. "Ah, there it lies. This entire city is collapsing around me. Love, marriage, children. It's ghastly. I may have to move to the continent."

"This is nothing romantic. Just art supplies. I can give you a small list."

Macauley blew a breath though his teeth, removed the cheroot, and tossed his scotch back. "Hildy will bash you over the head with her umbrella should she find out. The Shaw chit is one of hers now, you know that. The bloody Duchess Society. The American is in knee deep, God help her."

Chance couldn't stop himself from asking, a blunder he blamed on the scotch, "Have you ever felt something you didn't want to, Mac? Even once? Like you stumbled across a treasure in the most unexpected place?"

"Under someone's skirt, you mean? Sure, lots of treasure to be found there." But his gaze immediately skipped across the ballroom, defying his indifference. Chance followed it only to find the Duke of Leighton's sister, Lady Philippa, standing by the window, plotting her escape. Blond, beautiful, and animated in a way that drew a man's attention, she was dangerous. A reckless chit who pretended not to be. The worst kind. Too *everything* for Xander Macauley, a blackguard who would never be allowed near her.

It would be irony of a sort if *that* was the chit who brought him down.

Leighton and Macauley were friends, of sorts. If you counted being thrown in the Thames as friendship, which had happened last year. Leighton the one doused, Macauley the one standing on the riverside laughing. But Macauley going after Lady Philippa would ruin everything. The man couldn't be that foolish.

Chance peered into his glass, wishing for more alcohol. "I guess your silence means no."

"Send me the list of supplies you need," Macauley growled and strode away, headed to the drink cart in the corner.

Leaving Chance to watch his bogus governess twirl in the arms of her betrothed.

Franny was starving. Lightheaded, her stomach growling incessantly.

She wasn't used to going hours without a bite to eat.

But she'd followed the modiste's advice, and her borrowed gown had held.

After being escorted back to Rose Hill by Tobias Streeter and his contingent, she headed directly for the kitchen—and the plate of lemon scones she'd spied before leaving. Shrugging from her coat only to find Chance Allerton sprawled on the bottom step of his grand staircase like an expectant father.

He'd been at the ball, studying her from the perimeter of the dance floor much like he was now. Emotion she couldn't discern lighting his vivid blue eyes. She'd heard the whispers about him. He'd refused to waltz, angering every ravenous mother in attendance, then rudely disappeared. There were numerous theories about where he'd gotten off to. A new mistress, a card game in a back parlor, a brawl with his hoodlum friends, but near the truth of possibly being sick of occupying a room swarming with sycophants.

Franny hated to admit it, but she'd felt a burst of relief at seeing Lady Chapman-Holmes in the crowd after Remington left. He wasn't with his old mistress. However, he could have been attending a *new* one.

She was jealous... but no one needed to know.

He glanced up as she halted at the staircase. Close enough to catch the scent of bergamot clinging to his skin, the faint hint of scotch riding the air. His hair was a gorgeous disaster, disheveled from handling. His cravat untied, the ends dangling down his chest. His jacket tossed over the banister, shirt undone enough to expose his collarbone. Sleeves rolled to his elbows, exposing muscular forearms that almost no man in the *ton* could claim. He'd gone from masterfully attired to lord of a country manor in a blink.

She didn't have to try hard to imagine him with no clothing whatsoever. Another of her secrets. She had a vibrant imagination where he was concerned.

"Katherine is asleep in the nursery. Your companion is with her, on a settee that looks to be barely holding her. I think, despite her frightening demeanor, she's actually good with children."

"She's very good with children. She's simply not good with men."

Chance's brow rose, waiting for her to say more, so she didn't.

Finally, he scrubbed his hand over his mouth, tilting his head, thinking. "You're going to marry him, then. It looked quite official on the ballroom floor. Hillsdale had a look of complete ownership on his face. Should I offer congratulations?"

A wave of lightheadedness hit her, and Franny swayed, reaching for the newel post. Her bonnet tumbled to the floor. Chance was on his feet instantly, grasping her shoulders. She shook her head, embarrassed, trying to sidestep his bruising hold. Yanking her coat from her arms, he tossed it over the banister alongside his.

"I haven't eaten. This dress. It's Hildy's, and the modiste implied my ample curves would bust the seams if I consumed so much as even one biscuit."

With a harsh oath, his hand trailed down her arm, leaving fire in its wake. Clasping her fingers, he led her down the hallway, thankfully toward the kitchen. He linked his with hers, the first time she'd held hands with a man in her life. "Your body is a bloody fantasy, don't let anyone tell you differently."

She stumbled along behind him, her breath caught in her chest. *Fantasy.* She'd never been anyone's fantasy.

Well past midnight, the kitchen was deserted when they entered it. Only the scent of grilled meat and stewed cabbage remained. Lighting a candle, then a wall sconce, Chance pulled out a chair from a scuffed table the scullery staff used for meals. "Turn," he ordered after she sat. Too hungry to argue, she swiveled, presenting her back.

From the first touch, she couldn't have said a rational word had her life depended on it.

He was efficient. Obviously well acquainted with the intricacies of women's attire. Easily undoing the top two buttons of her gown, allowing her to breathe without constraint. He wore no gloves, and his calloused fingertips sent trails of heat whispering through her.

The man worked with his hands, and it showed.

He paused, a sigh slipping free, his body towering over her. She was thankful she couldn't gaze into his face from this position. "If you were truly my governess, I wouldn't be this familiar. Not that I should, in any case. But we're friends more than the other, I suppose. Employer and such. I wanted you to know." Stepping back, he swore beneath his breath, his hands dropping from her. "I'm not, that is, I've never taken advantage of someone vulnerable."

Her heart skipped a beat because a man had once taken advantage of her vulnerability. "You've never had to. They come to you." She glanced over her shoulder, letting him know she appreciated his honesty. And that she was teasing.

Startled, he blinked and stepped back, bumping into the cupboard. Lips curving in self-mockery, he began assembling the items to make tea. *Tea.* Her fascination blossomed in the cozy confines of his decaying estate's kitchen—as she watched an honorable viscount trying desperately to *prove* he was honorable.

No one had believed him before, she guessed.

In less than a minute, he delivered a plate piled high with cheese, ham, and the lemon scones she'd spied earlier, followed soon by a cup of tea, steam lifting free to tickle her nose. Then he sprawled in the opposite chair, his own cup cradled in his broad palms. The tip of his boot edged her ankle, and they shifted in their seats to adjust, gazes downcast.

She took a sip of excellently brewed tea and dug into the ham. "You're quite handy in the kitchen, my lord," she murmured, chewing as delicately as a ravenous person could.

"Destitution requires a man to prepare his own meals. My funds only allow for service at breakfast and lunch." He sipped, his cobalt gaze striking hers over the rim of his cup. "You've never had a viscount wait on you before? Is that what I'm hearing?"

"I've never had *any* man wait on me."

Her words registered in a way she hadn't intended. The chemical charge that traveled between them whenever they were in the same space crackled like lightning. His pupils expanded, a muscle in his jaw starting to tick. Seconds passed while they breathed softly in the winter twilight.

Finally, in tense silence, he reached for a scone. Then turned it in his hand like he didn't know what to do with it.

"You don't like Hillsdale." Dusting a crumb from her bottom lip, she tried to ignore the way his gaze tracked the movement. But her body clenched, seeing everything her mind sought to repel.

He shook his head, biting into the scone. His hair glimmered, amber threads sparking in the candlelight. Grainy stubble dotted his cheeks, giving him the look of a swashbuckler. Both elegant and ferocious. And beautiful, even if she wished he wasn't. "No, more like I feel you're selling yourself to the lowest bidder."

"I don't have the luxury to be selective. My father will disown me. He's threatened, and I believe him. We're not close. We never have been. A woman alone, without funds, can't survive in this world." Glancing at her plate, she decided to be honest. Flickering candlelight and the gentle rumblings of a slumbering house made it seem as if they were the only two people in England. "I made a mistake a year ago that limits my negotiating power."

He looked up, arrested. Swallowing, he placed his cup on the table. "A mistake."

She traced a crack in the plate with her pinkie, avoiding his gaze. "The kind that men can make every day, but a woman never can. Not even a hint of one. He was cruel, and I was foolish. Other than that, it's in the past."

He sat back, his chair squealing in protest. Such a broad body housed in a threadbare piece. He must have hated it when he designed the most gorgeous furniture. "So that's why you're running." His words were edged with anger. She wasn't sure where they were directed.

Her temper sparked when she had no reason to be incensed. "I'm *not* running. I would have stayed despite the scandal. It only ruined my chances of a proper marriage in Philadelphia. High society, they call it there. Nothing so graceful as the *ton*. An entanglement I never desired anyway. I could have lived as a spinster without issue. I want to, in fact."

His lips parted, closed, then parted again. He fiddled with his cup before grabbing another scone. She'd never known a man to consider *her* opinion before imposing his own. "What about love?"

The sip of tea she'd taken went down too fast. She coughed and dropped a slice of cheese to her plate. "*Love?*"

"You don't believe in it?"

She coughed again, struggling to take a full breath. "Yes, of course. Well... perhaps." She dusted a crumb from her plate. Shrugging, she knocked her knees together beneath the table. "I'm not sure."

He tilted his head, a charming habit she'd noticed he made when he was thinking. "I've seen it, you see. Living proof. Tobias Streeter and Hildy, a woman I believed would never get twisted up, are in deep, sickening love. From the first moment, too. The Duke of Markham and his duchess, Georgiana, the same. Have you taken a look at those two? They went sneaking off tonight to a back parlor or something. They can't keep their hands off each other, and they have *children*."

Franny pretended extreme interest in the border of lilies circling her plate. She couldn't look into Chance Allerton's indigo eyes and talk about *this*. "I find this a little hard to believe coming from the biggest rake in London. Lord tup-'em-and-leave-'em."

"That moniker is absurd. And untrue. My relationships are entered into with full knowledge regarding my expectations. *And* hers. Breaking someone's heart, if that's possible, isn't my goal. I only want the moment of solace the connection brings."

She sniffed. *Men*. With women, it was never that simple.

"Listen here, sweetheart, I *could* believe in it," he said, his voice rising. "More than you seem to be able to."

Her smile was unexpected and undeniable. *Sweetheart*. She couldn't stop herself from lifting her gaze. He had a scowl on his face and was staring at his scone like it held answers to life's questions. "What about marriage then?"

"What about it?" he growled, taking an angry bite.

She pointed. "Your leaking roof. Your housekeeper's bad tooth. The vicar's home in the village that needs renovations. You have to marry. You need funds. Blunt, as the English say. Are you telling me you require *love* before you'll do it? I've been in this country six months, my father talking nothing *but* marriage, and I've never heard love mentioned once. Except by Hildy Streeter, and I agree, she's too over the moon for her husband to pay any attention to."

"Thanks for the reminder of the dismal state of my affairs." With a grunt, Chance rose from his chair and began riffling through the cupboard. Locating a dusty liquor bottle on the back shelf, he turned with a grin that sent her stomach to her knees. He was unfairly, unjustly handsome, the bounder. "I'm not following my parent's example. I bloody refuse. They hated each other and made life miserable for anyone around them." Pouring a measure into his empty teacup, he lifted a brow. "I can't guarantee the quality, but it's likely to warm the soul."

She finished her tea, then held out her cup. Her hand was trembling. Perhaps not enough for him to notice. The brandy *was* abysmal, but it did the job as it trailed down her throat.

"You could be right. Maybe fancying a chit is enough."

Her heart gave a leaden thump. Franny didn't actually want to talk Viscount Remington into marrying someone who—she could admit in the depths of her mind—wasn't *her*. "Fancy," she said with a false laugh. "Such an English way of putting it. So delicate."

"When it's not delicate," he murmured, his eyes glowing. "Not at all."

Franny slid her cup to the table, her mind whirling with lewd images. A mysterious thread in his tone was lighting a fire inside her. She shifted to find a position that relieved the pulse settling fast and hard between her thighs.

He sighed, his eyes closing. "You're supposed to hide what you're feeling right now, Francine Shaw."

"Why?" she whispered.

"Because it tempts a man beyond measure, sweetheart." He leaned in, letting her see the same on his face. His cheeks were flushed, his breaths coming in shallow bursts. "Passion is different from love. Don't confuse them. I never have."

She slid closer until her bottom was on the edge of her seat, helpless to deny her attraction. She'd never been a good liar. The scent of raw wood drifted to her, mixing with the pleasing kitchen aromas. He'd apparently been working before she arrived.

"Is that what you did before?"

She licked her lips, a band tightening around her chest. "I never felt this for him. For anyone, I think I'm realizing. Never experienced... *passion*."

He flattened his hand to the table, his knuckles paling. It provoked her to see his reaction, even if she wasn't sure what she was doing to cause it. "Do you want to tell me about it?"

Someday, she thought but didn't say it.

That life seemed like another now. Another time and place. This room, this estate, this *man* was all she wanted at the moment. In mere days, she was leaving for a new one.

Her now was *his*.

Chapter Eight

Where a Viscount Learns Lessons in Love

With an oath, he was out of his chair, sending it to the floor with a bang.

He dropped to his knees before her, studying her stunned expression like he would a diagram of one of his designs. His hand went to cradle her cheek. Her skin was soft, creamy, glowing in the candlelight. Her lips parted, inviting him to touch her. He didn't understand why he wanted her with such intensity. Stronger than he recalled yearning for another human being. "I'm going to kiss you, sweetheart. Senseless, if I can manage it. Stop me now if that's not what you want."

She reached and, instead of pushing him away, wrapped her hand around his wrist and held him to her. "I haven't agreed to any agreements. This is *my* life. Until I leave Derbyshire, it's my life. You're only taking what I want to give. There is no betrayal or confusion on my part."

He closed in until his lips brushed hers. She tasted of tea and lilies, lemon and life. "Your choice then."

She hummed a *yes* and slanted her head, seizing his lips when he would have moved in gradually. Awkward, eager, remarkable. Her hunger palpable, wrapping him in gossamer strands of longing.

She was untried but not.

Tangling her hand in his hair, she slid forward, sending his body rocking back. Her breasts were full and warm against his chest. Her bountiful body within reach for the first time. Weakened, he parted his lips, engaging her tongue in play. Showing her. *This. And this.* She moaned, the ragged vibration trailing from his mouth directly to his hardening cock.

Without hesitation, she followed his guidance until they found a faultless fit. That moment when a kiss climbs a mountain, soars away from the people initiating it, and into the heavens. Two becoming one.

Take, his mind shouted. *Take her.*

Show her how wonderful it can be.

Her hairpins were easily removed until her glorious strands filled his fist. His other hand going to her waist, fingers curling around her hip in possession, bringing her off the chair and against him.

On their knees, they worshiped. She was on a quest to destroy—even if she didn't know it. She handled him greedily, exploring. Smiling against his lips when he groaned low in his throat at her aggression.

The sensation was dizzying. Of being seduced. Coerced. Splendidly manipulated. When that had always been *his* role. This witty, kind, intelligent American hellion was diminishing his prior experiences until they were muted images and nothing more.

She was making him forget everything but her.

The ground shifted beneath his feet, around his heart, in ways he wasn't ready to allow. Because something about this—about *her*—felt *right*.

Which scared the shite out of him.

Taking her face in his hands, he wrenched back, their breath pelting each other's cheeks. "We'd better stop, Franny. I'm losing my list of reasons for *not* taking you upstairs and discovering your incredible body on a medieval bed the size of a small village."

She smirked, a cagey bit of feminine persuasion that had his cock threatening to make choices for him. Dusting her thumb across his lower lip, she added a nibble to seal the deal. "Do you want to stop? I don't."

Rising, he yanked her up and stepped between her legs. His hand cupped the back of her head, bringing her lips to his. The kiss immediately tumbled into that magnificent spot it would never leave—not as long as they continued.

For years. Forever.

The intimate, lush space they'd created. The *us*.

Dazed, he roped his arm around her waist and lifted her to the balls of her feet. His shaft met the molten valley between her thighs in a grinding, elemental, age-old dance. She clutched his shoulder, hand curving around the nape of his neck, urging him closer. Mating with clothing rumpled but in place.

He wasn't unfastening more buttons on her gown, he *wasn't*. Even if he wanted to more than he wanted to get his desk into bloody Carlton House.

Losing patience, his skin starting to tingle, he walked her back until she hit the wall, his lips sliding down her jaw as he pressed his hips to hers. He would *die* for her body. Throw himself before her and *beg* for... one... taste. Imagining her naked, and that's what he was doing, brought him closer to doom. Sparks lit behind his lids as she wiggled against him, his cock finding a delightful temporary home nestled between her thighs.

He had the sensation. The I-could-come-soon buzz from nothing more than a kiss. Grabbing her hips, he let her feel everything she was doing to him, unable to hide his need. Unable to do a damned thing but want her.

Her head dropped back, a sigh ripping free. "*Remington.*"

"Chance, remember?" he murmured, his breath a tender burn over her skin. "Remington was my father."

She pulled back enough to stare into his eyes. Hers were wide and such a vibrant golden hue it took his breath. "Only your friends call you Chance."

He touched his brow to hers, willing his heart to slow. "How good"—he swallowed, a loud click in the night—"a friend do you want to be, Franny Shaw?"

She gazed at him, candlelight creating magic. Bathing them in gilded awareness. Desire and inevitability converged, a blistering shroud. "I want to sketch you in that medieval bed the size of a small village. You promised I could, after all." She caught the edge of his mouth with her tongue, seeking admission. Rough, unsteady, and devastating. "*After*," she whispered, her voice cracking with desire.

Chance's hand closed into a fist at her hip. Drawing her skirt up, he tried valiantly not to imagine what lay beneath.

Although he was losing the battle.

He wanted her to leave this night believing she couldn't live without him. "You know what you're asking?"

For the space of a second, she looked uncertain. More understanding than he wished she had flashing across her face. Then the passion they generated floated back in, erasing her unease. "I know. And since you're being a gentleman and asking, I'm saying yes."

"I'm asking," he murmured hoarsely, took her hand, and dragged her from the room.

Franny thought to tell him she had experience. A little.

To ease his concern. Because he glanced back twice as he hauled her along the darkened corridors, indecision marking his features. A slight frown dancing in and out of candlelight. His features starkly stunning, reminding her why she'd wanted to capture them on paper. Indecision even as his shaft jutted beneath the fine wool of his trousers, proof of his yearning. There was simply no way to conceal it, especially when it had been pressed like a stone against her hip.

Franny smiled tenderly. She was going to touch him. *Soon.*

And then she would fill a thousand canvases with his image.

She would discover what she'd missed before. When she'd let curiosity and a half-attraction mistakenly lead her to a man's bed. A man she'd assumed *liked* if not loved her. A man who had been her friend. A man who had falsely said no one else would want her.

But *this* man wanted her. So, she was letting him take her.

They stumbled down passageways, taking turns until she lost her way. Up a narrow, winding servant's stairwell. Curving, curving. Where she finally stopped him, taking the higher step and his lips in a bruising kiss because she couldn't *not*. A persistent pulse began to beat between her thighs, a rush of blood through her head. For the first time, she believed she was going to experience pleasure with someone, not merely her forlorn touch in the darkness of her bedchamber.

Chance moaned in silent, unwitting agreement, lingering, his touch trailing from her waist to her shoulders. Along every curve, and she possessed a few. Back to her breasts, where he filled his hands, his thumbs snaking over her nipples.

What he could locate beneath layers—layers she wanted *gone*.

Their harsh exhalations filled the confined space, echoes reverberating as she yanked his cravat free and let it flutter to the stairs.

Pulling himself from the kiss, he crouched to retrieve the strip of silk, then continued up, his fingers linked with hers. "We're not tupping on the staircase, my eager girl." He glanced over his shoulder, his gaze molten. "And yes, it's possible. Not comfortable perhaps... but possible. Maybe someday, I'll show you. Now, we need a bed."

Then conversely, he made the trip to his chamber a challenging journey.

Stopping her at the top of the stairs, at each doorway they passed, a meandering, passionate exploration that carried them in circles down the hallway. As if he couldn't go two steps without touching her. Working the buttons on the back of her gown until it hung off her shoulders. His cravat lost. A button on his shirt tumbling away from them and across the faded runner.

When they made it to his bedchamber, it was madness. She didn't even stop to examine his personal space for the clues she desperately wanted to grasp about him.

Wrapping her in his arms, he kicked the door closed and murmured words she didn't comprehend against her neck. His breath was sweet and hot, scorching her to her bones. He moved away only long enough to awkwardly remove his boots while she toed off her slippers. Then they challenged each other with snickering, gasping pleas

71

and gazes that singed the air. Clothing became a puddle at their feet. Shirt, trousers, drawers. Gloves, gown, chemise, stays, stockings.

When they were done, they stood, panting, gazes roaming. There had not been time to look at the man she'd chosen to initiate her before. He hadn't allowed it. And she'd been too apprehensive to ask. Fumbling in the dark, pain, then him leaving the bed to put on his trousers.

Chance Allerton allowed her curiosity free rein.

After a languid journey along the muscle and sinew of his finely toned body, she met his gaze. He had the physique of an active man. Unlike anyone she'd yet seen in the *ton*.

His throat worked, his lids fluttering, his breath slipping out in a rush. "You're the most stunning woman I've ever seen. And *bloody hell*, I really thought I knew what to expect."

She started to argue, tell him he was mistaken. That *he* was the beautiful one. But he shook his head, backing her into the bed before she could. Where she went down. And he crawled over her.

She stopped him, hand on his chest.

He looked up, through a swing of tangled, damp dark-as-midnight hair. "Is this too fast?" His shoulders rose and fell. "Stop me. Tell me no."

She giggled, trailing her finger down his chest to his belly. His muscles quivered beneath her palm. His cock was jammed between them, against her thigh, hard and hot. It twitched with his effort to hold himself back. She wanted to wrap her hands around it but wasn't sure if she should. "I merely wanted a moment to look. I'm going to capture you on paper, like I've wished to for *months*. I'm as enthralled with your body as you are with mine. I want to remember."

His smile was glorious, softening his features, a sweetness that made her heart stutter. His eyes shimmered in the dim light, inviting her in. "There's no bloody way that could be true, sweetheart. My adoration is fierce. More than I've felt in my life. Yours can't compare, though I'm thankful for it."

Then, he took her under. Weight pressing her into the mattress. Braced on his forearms, he kissed her hungrily, his hand finding her breast, his thumb her hardened peak. Circling, palming, until she lost reason entirely, her head rolling to the side. She arched into him, seeking more. Perhaps she even whispered it. Her body was melting, racing away from her and toward him.

With a muffled groan, he caressed his way down her body.

Sensation exploded as his lips circled her nipple, rolling it gently between his teeth. "Shall I make you come like a proper Englishman, my American jewel? Very thorough but at a dignified pace. The English disposition is good for something, I suppose."

He notched himself between her legs, working his hips from side to side. Deliberately, until her vision blurred. Dear heaven, she'd never imagined this was a whole-body experience. Skin slick from exertion, bodies grinding like they were polishing stone. Lifting her leg high on his hip, he leaned over her, working one breast, then the other with his lips and fingers.

"I have one question." He blew a purposeful breath over the now-sizzling nub, making her gasp. His hand snaked between their bodies, fingers dancing south. Between her thighs, parting her folds, he slid a finger gently inside. Stroking tenderly as she sighed, hips lifting. Deeper, then deeper still. "Would you like to crest the first time with my cock inside you or my tongue?"

Grasping the counterpane as he began to pump his hand, she whispered hoarsely, "Cock first, tongue after. If I'm allowed both. Then sketching, like you promised."

She realized he'd halted, his movement stilling. Soaring from the passionate sea he'd tossed her into, she opened her eyes to find his expression filled with disbelief. A howling gust of wind rattled the windowpanes as they stared. His lips parted, but it was a minute before any words came out.

"Where did you come from, Francine Shaw? You're my dream come to life. Such. A. *Dream.* I fear if I touch you, you'll disappear, a misty yearning deep in my soul evaporating into the night."

She raised to her elbow and reached for his shaft, wrapping her hand around him. Hard, smooth, sleek. He was beautiful, ravenous, cheeks flushed, skin moist. He moaned softly, his lids quivering. "Stay."

"I'm not going anywhere, Chance."

With a sigh, he tore into her. The kiss feral, then he was gone, sliding down her body for real this time. Caressing her ribs, her belly, the side of her breast. While pumping his finger in long, sluggish strokes inside her, seeking to drive her mad.

Although she'd asked for the other first, he moved between her legs, nipping her hipbone, his bristly cheeks grazing her thighs, his mouth delving between her moist folds until she arched and moaned, turning into someone she didn't recognize. He took the pebbled bit of hidden flesh between his lips and sucked, groaning into her skin, his own pleasure breaking the surface. His tongue and finger worked in tandem, in a coordinated, furious pace. She cried out. There was no way to contain her rapture, the sound and scent of them infusing the air.

A rush of sensation crept from the base of her spine, threatening to consume her. Curling her toes, her fingers going into fists, her body arching.

In moments, she was coated in dew, heat, arousal. Wrapped up and around him. Mindless, starved for pleasure. For him.

"*Now*," she said and lifted her hips, needing, wanting. Begging. She wanted him to take her to that place. Now. Now. *Now*.

"Look at me," he murmured against her thigh, his tongue drawing a maddening, lazy circle. "A sketch for your collection. Or maybe we'll make art right here. I'll trace on your bare skin with my fingertips and solve for the complexities of the design with my tongue."

She followed orders—and knew she'd never forget the sight of Chance Allerton stretched across the bed, his muscled arms wrapped around her legs, his dark head resting between her thighs. She should have been embarrassed. When all she felt was a nagging sense of rightness and humbly fragile ownership.

She didn't want him to do this with another woman. *Ever*. That wish was clear.

The wind whipped against the windows, howling, drowning out their staggered breaths.

Growling faintly, he nipped her thigh, her belly, levering on his forearms and rising over her. His fingers leaving her only to nudge his shaft into place at her entrance. "You are delectable. I hardly know how to contain my avarice. An unfamiliar occurrence. A gift delivered to my doorstep that I'm bloody accepting even if I shouldn't."

She arched her hips, seeking. "Quit talking," she rasped against his neck when he lowered himself over her. His delicious weight sinking them into the mattress. "Start doing."

Laughing, he grasped her arm and pinned it over her head, sampling the hard nipple thrust against his cheek by the movement. "What a little bulldog you are. My gorgeous American bulldog."

"I know what I want." She angled his mouth back to hers. "Why act like I don't? I don't understand that about this country. Every desire hidden beneath a thousand layers of dread."

"Why, indeed." Sighing raggedly, he accepted her offer, kissing her while he nudged his shaft between her slick folds, then with a jolt, sliding inside her. A gradual possession. Measured. Determined. Filling her, changing her. Rocking movements that she caught on to quickly.

It was the most natural of unnatural performances. Addictive from the start. She closed her eyes to the glory, skin tingling, air trapped in her lungs. Positioning her bent leg against his hip, he shifted and eased deeper into her, the push and pull lighting a fire inside her.

More *and* less as he stroked. Waging a war. To go faster, to linger. To speed up, to slow. He got her close to a summit, her brusque entreaties filling the silence, the creak of the bed marking their tempo, then he paused, murmuring profane suggestions in her ear. Every one of them—bending her over his desk, having her ride him, filling her again and again—increased the delight she chased. Until she was bound to him, a quivering, helpless mass of nerve endings.

She caught his shoulder, his jaw. Fingers tangling in his hair. Nails digging into the band of muscle around his forearms. Urging him, biting him, hips lifting, bumping in a synchronized cadence.

It was brutal, magnificent elegance.

Sensation gathered, and this time, he let it build. Rocking from tip to base, fully owning her. Entrenched as far as possible one moment, almost sliding out the next. His arms trembled where he held himself over her. Dropping his brow to her shoulder, he took gasping breaths and murmured lost bits of nothing in her ear.

"Close," he said, the word wrenched from him. "*Close.* Come with me."

She shook her head wildly, unable to reply. Unable to do more than move with him, hold him, possess him as he possessed her. Swearing beneath his breath, his hand slipped between their bodies, grazing the swollen nub just above where he penetrated her.

Circling, pressing, demanding her release.

It was enough. Too much. *Everything.*

He knew exactly how to touch her, exactly what she needed.

Finally, splendidly, her climax ripped through her. Dimming her vision, snatching her breath. Her hands flew to the counterpane, fisting, body bowing. Her cry was savage, and he seized her lips, swallowing the sound lest it rouse the household.

He tangled himself around her, grinding, moist skin and fury, his release claiming him. They gasped and panted, bumped and shifted, sighs, groans, murmurs filling the dark night. Drawing forth every last bit of pleasure.

Finally, his weight settled upon her in surrender.

It was the most animalistic experience of her life. Incredible and tumultuous. She felt turned inside out, like a piece of clothing ripped from one's body.

She was ruined. In the best way possible.

"Remy," she murmured against his temple, a bead of sweat streaking down his jaw to her cheek.

He took her with him when he rolled away, tucking her against his side. His lips dusted her brow, a haphazard caress. His chest rose and fell in a mad rhythm. "Remy," he repeated in a sleepy, sated murmur. Stretching, he sighed in gratifying contentment and hugged her close.

She sought to ask him if lovemaking was always like this.

Life-altering. Crushing. So, so beautiful.

Adorable, troublesome man, exhaustion claimed him before she could.

Chapter Nine

Where a Recalcitrant Viscount Broods

"Why are you so grouchy?"

Chance bit into an apple he'd pilfered from the kitchen during his foray for food and art supplies an hour ago, chewing slowly. He was trying to come to grips with the sentiments swirling through him—and the effort was affecting his mood. He'd never been much for Christmas, and here it was, dawn of a new one. And his emotions were tangled in knots. "Is that the American term for vexed? Who says I'm grouchy?"

Franny smiled, a winsome, knowing curve of her lips and licked her thumb, then swiped it across a stroke she'd drawn on the page.

Chance's belly quivered, his fingers curling around the fruit. Discomfited, he glanced to the window. They had at least two hours before daybreak, when she'd need to return to her chamber. Katherine would be up soon after, excited about the holiday, and her governess couldn't be found sketching the master of the house in his drawers.

The artist in a ripped chemise and nothing else. Her hair untamed, flowing down her shoulders and back in a crimson-threaded bounty. Her nipples, which he'd found were the shade of a dusky sunset, straining against silk and calling to him to suck them. The bed behind them an utter disaster. The room smelling marvelously of carnal delight.

He'd bottle the scent if he could. Lifting his hand to his nose, he drew her—*them*—in.

"You should be happy," she said cheerfully and drew a swift set of lines, glancing at him once to make sure she was capturing him correctly. "I did what you asked. Now you do what *I* ask. Getting you on paper is why I ended up here, you know. This was the deal. Consider this my Christmas present. I want to capture that little crook on your nose. The scar on your lip. That lank of hair that juts out no matter how hard you try to contain it."

He sank back against the settee, vanquished. Trying very diligently to avoid looking at the dark thatch of hair between her thighs. Flattered to his soul that she'd studied him so well. And feeling a bit clever that he had her a *true* present shoved in his cupboard across the way. She *had* done what he asked. The second time. When he'd awoken to find her circling his nipple with her fingernail. Climbed atop him without a hint of apprehension, in fact. Worked his shaft inside her with only the slightest clumsiness. How his thumb had ended up between her lips, he couldn't say. Just the tip, a gentle suck and nip. He'd about come then and there.

Since when did he like *that*?

Breasts bouncing, calling him Remy in that breathy voice. In crisis mode, he'd flipped her over and resorted to some fancy finger work to make sure she came before he did.

"Quit fidgeting, my lord."

"I said I would pose. I'm posing."

Pose. Bloody hell, was he in deep trouble with this chit.

Her gaze flicked up, taking him in. She was resting against an armchair enough of a distance away to keep him from easily touching her. With his toe if he stretched perhaps. Her eyes were a painfully vivid shade of gold. Her cheeks ruddy from stubble-burn, lips plump from abuse. He let his attention meander down her body. Amazing breasts, slender, graceful feet—and everything in between made for pleasure. Made for *him*. She really was unfairly endowed.

Duly appreciative, he wanted her with an intensity he'd never imagined. Not since his boyhood had he been less in control.

With her soft smiles and tender touches, she made his world shrink until it was merely them filling it. When he'd always occupied the largest, loneliest of worlds.

The difference between lust and love circled, bringing a leaden ache to his chest. A tightness to his breathing. A clamminess to his skin.

How to tell, he wondered? How to tell?

Because he feared this was happiness he was suffering from, or more confusing, contentment. Of that, he was fairly bloody sure. Bits of the wall he'd built around his heart tumbled when she was near, the barricade getting lower and lower. Like she'd taken a pickax to it.

"Are you still planning to marry him?" he asked without strategy. The thought of her with another man made him want to put his fist through a wall. His emotions were under siege, like he was preparing for a round at Gentleman Jackson's. Seconds from being punched in the face. Or the gut. When he'd never been covetous of a woman. Never trotted himself out like that, vulnerable and unsure.

And there had been many women. An unwarranted number he couldn't now recall.

Her charcoal skidded across her sheet, but she didn't look up. "Are you offering another solution?"

He took a vicious bite of the apple, his gaze roving to the ceiling. Spiderwebs and cracks. Faded wallpaper. Leaky roof. Rose Hill was tumbling down around him. He needed funds. Franny Shaw was wealthy. She understood his vision, was becoming a helpmate. He'd never met a woman who shared his passion for design or one who even *had* a passion outside him. She was an artist, talented and incredible.

And *bloody hell*, did he want her. Insanely. Criminally.

But he'd promised himself long, long ago. Promised that boy. No marriage without love.

"I didn't think so," she murmured.

"I don't have all the answers, you know."

She hummed a raw, jittery sound. "You don't seem to have any."

He dropped his head back to the settee with a sigh. "I knew this was going to happen if I touched you. But I couldn't *not* touch you. And you didn't say no when you bloody well could have! I would have gone crawling back to my bedchamber and pleasured myself all night while thinking about you, yes, but at least we'd be safe."

She rose, crouching before him in that diaphanous chemise that provided absolutely no protection against his hunger. He glanced at the sketchpad, his chest tightening. A reflection of a man in the midst of indecision stared back at him. How honestly she saw him took his breath away.

"There was a man. In Philadelphia. A family friend. He didn't force me. I don't want you to think it was any choice but my own. My mistake, the way I term it. A mistake that became known because he let it be known, necessitating my leaving America. Anyway, he was cruel after. And during, now that I have..." Her smile was splendid despite the conversation. "Now that I have another experience to compare. He made me feel no one else would want me, so I took his offer. I was naïve, and he was heartless. It happens to women every day. I realize my foolishness isn't novel."

Chance cradled her jaw, drawing her lips to his. She went willingly. The kiss was tender and much less than he wanted to share. And much more. "He was a *fool*. You're my fantasy, my dream. I wish I'd been your first everything."

Touching her brow to his, she whispered, "I could help you with your designs more easily if you talked to me. This passing notes back-and-forth nonsense isn't aiding the process."

Chance dusted his lips beneath her ear. "Our current state of undress is why I resorted to this nonsense."

Sitting back, she drew a languid circle on his belly with her charcoal.

He grabbed the pencil and tossed it aside, rolling her over on the carpet. Where they kissed, touched, moaned. Grappled for control before submitting.

He was going to make her come again before dawn.

Then she laughed, belly-deep and authentic, and he hesitated, startled. He'd never laughed in bed. Teased. Talked. He felt as if he'd plunged into a lake with no bottom. Braced on his arms over her, he stared into her face, questioning the thoughts circling his mind, his heart. She had a tiny birthmark on her temple he'd never noticed. Freckles on her nose. Flecks of amber in her eyes. His fingers trembled where he held her. "If I asked, would you say yes?"

Her cheeks paled, her hand falling from the nape of his neck to the floor. "But you said, you told me... you won't marry without love. Does that mean, are you saying—"

He popped his palm over her mouth before she could finish the question. A question he wasn't prepared to answer.

She sat up, breaking his hold. Her dejected expression breaking his heart. "No, then. I'd say no."

"Hillsdale? He gets a yes? When I get a no?" He gestured to the room they'd torn up in their passion, knowing he was being a jackass but unable to help himself. The fate of millions of asinine fools before him.

Franny scrambled to her feet, a woman on a rampage.

Chance's lips parted on a sigh. He'd never seen her angry—not truly—and a depraved part of him was aroused. Cheeks flushed, glorious breasts rising and falling beneath that twist of rumpled silk. Hips perfect for his hands to mold as he brought her against his body. *God*, he wanted to sink into her, make them forget about all this life shite.

Couldn't they simply get back to the basics?

"I can marry him knowing my father's money is all he's after. It's business. But not you, Remy."

"It isn't the money. We're friends. Or something lost in the chasm in-between that I can't for the life of me define. I only know that I'm trailing after you like a hungry hound, desperate for attention. But despite all that, despite my desire and my yearning, bloody hell if the blunt wouldn't help." He shoved to his feet, getting irritated himself. The viscountcy was not of his choosing, but he was trying to make the best of being saddled with it. Stalking across the room in search of his trousers, he found them in a wad under the bed, next to one of his boots.

"Have you seen this place?" he groused, jamming a leg into his pants and hopping around trying to secure the other. "My father left it in ruins. Left my family in ruins. My brother, Arthur, someday I'll tell you about his trials and my desperate effort to keep him on the straight and narrow. You want me to let Mrs. Walker's tooth fall out? The church roof to cave in? Oh, yes, they need a new one of those. I've got not only this estate and every member of the staff under my jurisdiction, but an entire village to worry over."

A gust of sour amusement left her lips. She was dancing about herself to get into her rig, a harder task than his. "Then find someone you don't fancy in *any* way to marry. You won't have questions in your eyes when you look at them. No woman wants to see those while in the midst of the act, my lord. Advice for your next encounter." She yanked her gown to her neck, the bodice gaping provocatively. To him at least. She had no hope to secure the thing without his assistance. "Don't judge the decisions I'm making, and I won't judge the ones *you're* making. The opera singer you engage in the new year will be your business and yours alone!"

He found his shirt draped across the escritoire and tunneled his arm in the sleeve. "How about this, sweetheart? You marry that pathetic example of baron manhood, but we continue to work together. We'll negotiate on a desk design some smog-filled morn in the near future, then I'll drag you upstairs for a quick tup. Because I won't be able to keep my damned hands off you if we're ever, *ever* in the same room."

Franny unsuccessfully fiddled with the buttons at the nape of her neck, her furious words lost. Although her caustic tone was clear. Holding her gown closed, she snatched up her sketchpad and charcoal, searching the room for the rest of her attire.

Chance sighed through his teeth and pointed. On the chair before the hearth. When he'd gone down for her art supplies, he'd found their clothing strewn about the house and collected everything in a tidy pile. Even her hairpins. He didn't want Mrs. Walker to find his cravat on the stairs and wonder what the hell had gone on the evening prior.

Although he wouldn't be surprised if Franny's shouts of ecstasy had traveled down the corridor and directly to her.

"Don't go," he blurted when she turned her back on him, realizing it was too late. Realizing they needed a bit of distance to think this through.

Last night was the most incredible of my life.

Nine words that whispered through his mind.

Nine words he couldn't release.

So, with a lingering glance filled with everything he'd lived his life without thus far, Franny was gone.

Leaving her stockings and one slipper but taking part of his heart.

Franny hobbled down the hallway to her bedchamber, through narrows bands of light and shadow. The rosewood paneling shone from a recent polishing she'd asked Mrs. Walker to organize. She wasn't going to cry, she thought and sniffled into the wadded coat pressed to her chest.

There was no need.

This wasn't like that last time, with Gerald Humbard III. Son of one of her father's business partners. Chance Allerton was turning her away out of panic, not callousness. The viscount was scared. She'd noted the emotion shimmering plainly in his cobalt eyes.

Only, she didn't know if she had the strength to fight him.

Thank goodness, she didn't encounter any of the pathetically modest staff currently employed at Rose Hill on her slog of shame. She opened her bedchamber door with a sigh that turned into a gasp the second she looked in the room.

Ada, mother of her heart, sat curled on the settee. A cup of tea in her hand, a wretched pout on her face. "Oh, my cheeky girl, have you flipped the wheels off the carriage this time."

Franny closed the door with a dull click and let the clothing she held tumble to the threadbare carpet. There was no way in Hades she could hide from the one person who, aside from a wayward viscount coming to know her well, knew her *best*. "I did possibly accede to another dreadful impulse."

"He won't marry you," Ada murmured and took a choked sip of tea. Like England, something she loathed. "Although I've seen the way he gazes at you. The way you gaze right back. Like two candles melting in the sun. Both when you think no one else is looking. But lust only creates trouble, dear heart. Never solves any in my humble experience. Your desire to sketch the man, don't argue because I know the way your mind works, has tossed us in the drink this time." She grunted and tapped the teacup's chipped rim against her teeth. "I suppose we must thank the heavens he's poor as a church mouse and can only employ three people who might have seen you. If your father should hear of this, we're doomed. I'll be living with my brother and his horrid wife before spring. Do you know what they're going to make me do with their children?"

Franny crossed to her vanity. The reflection displayed in the gilded mirror was a creature she didn't recognize. Rosy cheeks. Swollen lips. Eyes alight with feminine power. And, oh God, her hair. She tugged her hand through tangled strands that would have impressed Medusa. "He asked, actually."

In his roundabout, tiptoe fashion.

Franny knew it was absurd—but Chance Allerton's carefully veiled vulnerability made her want to pitch herself over the cliff into love with him. Foolish girl.

Ada's cup hit the table with a click. "He did *what?*"

Franny turned, clutching her gaping bodice. Plunking her bottom on the vanity's marble edge, she shrugged. "It was half-hearted. Hasty. Not insincere so much as rummaging for a solution to a tangle he's found himself mired in. Like a pig stuck in mud. It wasn't pretty or romantic."

"You said yes, of course." At Franny's silence, Ada's face paled and she slumped, head dropping to her hands. "A *viscount* who looks at you like he wants to eat you in one bite and go back for seconds. A man, a genuine one, obstinate and arrogant, but a *man*. When the lout your father has lined up is a boy. Please, dear girl, please tell me you said yes."

Franny shook her head. She wasn't selling herself to Viscount Remington. Baron Hillsdale, yes, *fine*. Baroness of naught, signed, sealed, and delivered. She'd never expected to have a *choice*. Her father had told her bluntly from the time she'd begun to attract masculine attention that she didn't.

But she would not, could not, start a life with a man who didn't want her when she suspected she was in love with *him*.

"You still plan to marry Hillsdale? After *this*?" She gestured to Franny's disastrous state.

A furious fire, unusual for her, sparked deep in Franny's belly. Like any woman, she could be a force when jammed into a corner. "We're purchasing each other. My money will be all Hillsdale's got any say over. The rest is mine to govern. I'll take my control where I can."

"As if life works that way." Ada released a scathing huff through her fingers. "What about the girl? If you decide to skip outta here before daybreak, which I think you should. What about that poor child?"

Franny pinched the bridge of her nose, tears stinging her eyes. *Kat*.

"You could take her to Hampton Hall until the new year. Mrs. Streeter invited us because she knew this silly farce of yours was going to blow like a faulty kettle. Her husband's estate is a twenty-minute carriage ride away. Inherited of a sort from Streeter's father, a viscount who didn't acknowledge him until the ancient sot was drawing his last. Unusual set of circumstances for a part-Romani bastard. Society can't decide whether to accept the man or not, and then he goes and marries an earl's daughter, making it an impossible situation. The English are a confounding lot. I swear to the ground they are."

"Lord Remington will come after me if I take Kat."

Ada lifted her head, her gaze narrowing in contemplation. Franny knew that look well, too well. The cleverness behind it had helped her avoid more than one scrape in her lifetime. "Not if we make it seem like it's a holiday invite you'd already accepted. A confused set of missives. Won't be the first time he's read about a woman's departure on a sheet of foolscap shoved beneath his door."

Franny pushed off the vanity, almost losing hold of her gaping gown. "I'm not setting up a race for the viscount to run like my prize mount. This isn't Epsom."

Ada beamed, smug and decided. Dusted her hands together as if she'd made a decision. "All's fair in love, isn't it? This lonely pile made even lonelier without women and children. A man thinks he wants his peace until he has it. The scorching glances the lord of the manor has been giving you could be close to love if you'd kick him across the ravine and into it. That you figured it out sooner can't be held against him. Men are senseless creatures."

Franny took a turn about the chamber, swiping her fingers across layers of dust on shelves, cracks in aged wallpaper, rips in an Aubusson rug that had once cost a fortune. Rose Hill made her want to weep. She would've happily sunk every penny of her dowry into the care and management of this estate, fallen in love with it right along with its owner. Become a mother to Kat.

The fact that she could so easily picture a life with them in this very house was unnerving.

Like most men, Chance Allerton was a ninnyhammer when it came to affairs of the heart. Franny dragged her bare toe across a ripple in the carpet, glancing to the window and the shades of blue and pink coloring a dawning horizon. A little push wasn't deceitful if the man in question was racing in that direction anyway, was it?

He *could* love her back. He'd stared into her eyes while he trembled, his broad body curving protectively around hers. His release frenzied... but his gaze calm. Sure. *Adoring*.

"I'll do it," Franny said, never considering that those were the exact words she'd spoken to Hildy Streeter to get her into this mess.

Chapter Ten

Where a Dejected Viscount Comes Calling

Franny had taken Kat's Christmas presents when she fled.

Which was fair as she'd purchased them.

He'd been determined the little girl would have her bloody gifts. But his absconding governess was one step ahead of him, never realizing she had gifts, too. Those damn art supplies Xander Macauley, true to his word, had delivered the night before. Chance had wrapped them in a length of tartan, one in his family for generations. Remnants of the lone, black Scottish mark on his mother's side and even included a crimson length of twine around the bundle that now looked ridiculous.

Or hopeful, depending upon one's perspective.

After Franny had bolted from his bedchamber the night before, in frustration, he'd finished sanding a desktop, then ridden his horse, Talbot, through the snow-capped fields until they were both panting from the effort. When he returned to Rose Hill at daybreak, his decision had been firmly in place. His mind calm. His body sated, thanks to a certain tenacious termagant's loving attention.

He'd only needed a few moments to search his heart, breathe deeply of the crisp winter air. And think.

Then he'd known.

Love. This was love he was feeling, blind and unrelenting.

For the woman *and* the girl.

He was giving in. Gladly giving *up* a life he didn't want for a new one he did.

He'd never felt the like, a sudden rush of emotion weakening his knees when a woman crossed within viewing distance. Her unique scent enough to have his heart skipping a beat. And... an *American.* This fact delighted him for many reasons it shouldn't. Her unsuitability made her perfect for *him.* He couldn't dictate the future, but he wanted Franny Shaw in his life. Wanted her laughter, her wit, her kindness raining down upon him.

Finally, he could picture someone when the word *viscountess* whispered through his mind. *Mine* traveling greedily behind it.

Perhaps the biggest surprise of all, he wanted to be a father to Kat. He wanted to fill Rose Hill with laughter and joy. Hers, to start. Then, the others to come.

With this certainty pillowing him like mist, he'd gone in search of his girls to find he had none in residence. Back to a lonely, creaking, dusty manor in the middle of Derbyshire. The dying pine branches attached to every available surface a reminder of his idiocy.

The answer was obvious. Franny deserved a sincere proposal.

Without questions in his eyes this time.

In a bit of a funk, he'd traipsed to his bedchamber, ignoring his disaster of a bed and the sensual aroma clinging to the air like a chill, and dug around in the side table, extracting his signet ring. It was temporary, of course. Until he had funds—*hers,* ironically—to purchase something more personal. However, he did quite like the scripted R circled by roses, modeled after the estate that had been in the Remington family for centuries. The small ruby he predicted would look stunning against her creamy skin.

She was extraordinary enough to appreciate it.

So here he stood on Tobias Streeter's country portico on Christmas morning, a gift for the woman who had led him on a merry chase to the very spot tucked awkwardly under his arm. Snow swirled inside the collar of his woolen coat, dusting his cheeks and brow. Chance rapped on the door of Hampton Hall once more, feeling the reverberation through the thick oaken slab. It was bloody freezing, and he was nervous.

Which made him annoyed and *more* nervous.

His situation worsened when the door was opened not by an aging majordomo, but Tobias Streeter himself, his canny grin saying things Chance didn't want to hear.

Macauley strode up behind his business partner, clapping his hands. "Before noon, I told you! The men in this circle are falling like diseased birds. You, the Duke of Markham, now Lord tup-'em-and-leave-'em. And for what? Bleeding *marriage*. Which I'm sick to stones of hearing about. Have to get rid of every mistress you've ever had, Remington, you understand that, right? The Duchess Society won't allow you to keep them. On a short leash forever, mate."

Tobias snaked his timepiece from his fob and flipped opened the silver case. "Shite on a shingle. Another ten minutes, and I would have won. And he won't miss the women. I've tried to tell you, Mac. If he found the right one, he'll only want her."

Skeptical, Macauley snorted around the cheroot dangling from his lips. "You owe me another ten, Street. He brought the bloody present. Didn't even try to save his dignity by sneaking in the domestics' entrance. Hands full of his embarrassment. Gads." He gestured to the tartan with a devilish smile. "Nice trimmings, mate. The American is going to slice that heart of yours into tiny pieces and wrap it up with that length of plaid."

While Tobias dug around in his trouser pocket for the wager he'd lost, Chance brushed past them, elbowing Macauley in the gut along the way.

Macauley rubbed his belly, the cheroot bobbing. "Is that what I get for delivering the best art supplies money can buy? German, those charcoals, not the pathetic English gear. And the drawing pad is *Italian* if you cared to notice. I called in a marker, a right fine one with a distributor of some very illegal but lucrative items, to get these on the quick. I've smuggled for the man for ten years now, and he's always owed *me*. Some show of friendship, this abuse, innit? And all to help another man walk the plank. I must be mad."

"Where is she?" Chance glanced around the deserted foyer, the sound of muted conversation and a child's laughter traveling down the corridor. He would thank his friend and thank him well, once he'd accomplished his mission.

Now that he knew he was sunk, he felt a dire need to share the news with the woman in question. *Immediately*.

Then Franny Shaw, God *love* her, did something that made everything *right*.

Made everything *perfect*.

In a fury, a blur of cream and gold, the scent of lilacs snaking into his soul, she was hugging him, his bundle of German and Italian regrets jammed between them.

His arm closed around her, bringing her as close as possible with the package between them.

Tears stung his eyes, lay thick in his throat.

She was a miracle he'd somehow stumbled upon. A rose in a field of weeds. The most exceptional person of his acquaintance. She and Kat the start of his family. Franny didn't care how her affection appeared to his friends. To society. She didn't mind that he was poor. That he'd fumbled the task of proposing the first time around, trying lamely to tell her he might love her. That he said silly things and acted like an arse half the time. She wasn't asking him to plead, grovel, beg. Or holding a grudge and causing him to apologize endlessly.

All things he would have done.

She only cared about him *showing up*.

He rather thought he could do that more often. Perhaps be an outstanding husband to match her brilliance if he worked hard enough. Aside from his furniture, he'd rarely been good at much of anything.

"You came," she whispered against his lips. Glancing down, she noticed the blunt end of a charcoal pencil sticking out of the tartan. "With presents. Oh, Remy, you darling, darling man! I didn't want to set up the race, such a foolish game, but I did, silly Ada, and you came."

"*Remy*," Macauley whispered in disgust as Tobias Streeter dragged him across the gallery, away from the embracing couple. "This is almost as tragic as you and Hildy."

"What race?" Chance asked, dipping his nose into her silken strands and breathing deeply for the first time in hours. Days. Years. Helplessly lost, his body beginning to react, he started calculating. One hour of gift-giving with the group, a brief luncheon, forty-five minutes tops, then when Kat went down for her nap, he would take Franny to the closest bedchamber or a linen closet even and—

"I recognize that look. *Later*," she whispered. "I'll leave my balcony door unlatched. I'm on the first floor, you can make it up, I'm sure. There's a very sturdy oak outside." She giggled and began to plunder the package, unfolding the tartan, sighing in delight at the offering. "This is the finest set of charcoals I've ever seen. German, *my*."

He stepped back, still holding the gift, as if he was watching a scene in a play. Sunlight, a rare, mid-winter burst, pierced the windows at her back, glazing her in radiance. Her eyes were a potent, golden hue, her hair shot through with amber. She was simply the best he could wish for in a life of broken promises, others and his own.

He wanted her in a multitude of ways with a fierceness that shook him. Curiously, most of them having nothing to do with his cock.

Wife. If she said yes, she would be his wife.

"We'll have to live here for a bit. Derbyshire, Rose Hill," he murmured instead of asking. A coward to the end. At least, this way, he could gain her initial response. "The city when we have to. House of Lords and all that bother."

"I'll go where you go," she returned, flipping through pages of a sketchpad that was, even he would admit, the most superb he'd seen outside an artist's salon. Macauley knew his smuggled products. "And Ada, of course. She'll learn to like you. Give her time. She and Kat are getting on so well. I'm overjoyed they seem to like each other."

"There's an easel on the way, too. Another week perhaps. A few more odds and ends." He shifted from boot to boot, looking for a place to set the bundle. His signet ring was burning a hole in his waistcoat pocket. "There's a parlor on the western side of the house that gets light throughout most of the day. Would make a decent studio of sorts. If you'd like." He settled her gift atop a mahogany sideboard, shoving aside the length of pine and holly serving as holiday décor. A pencil rolled free and bounced across the floor. He bent to pick it up, his back to her. "I even have a friend, a well-respected artist, who teaches classes. Only men, to date. I've already contacted him about working with you. I think he would, covertly because the world is not designed for women, once he sees your work."

"Chance. *Remy*. Look at me."

Setting the charcoal aside, he followed her directive. She'd come up behind him with a furtiveness that surprised him. The beat of his heart was drowning out the sounds of a holiday gathering rippling through the house, snatching his ability to take a full breath. "Do you have something to ask me?"

Her lips were curled at the edges. Delight and a hint of mischief transforming her face. For some reason, the latter gave him the courage to spill his secrets. Machiavellian tendencies, he understood. Could work with. That she wasn't the typical proper English miss perfected the moment. "The viscountess part won't be fun. I can guarantee that much," he mumbled and tunneled in his pocket. The signet ring was warm from its press against his chest.

Taking a breath, he presented it to her. A promise. A future. Like Macaulay had said, his heart for the taking. Possibly to be cut into slivers. "It's all I had time for. I'll find you the most glorious in London when we return."

Her smile grew to incredible proportions. She had the loveliest one he'd ever encountered. She slipped it on her ring finger, when he wore it on his pinkie, and the fit wasn't horrible. Not horrible at all. "I love it." She wagged her hand, catching a ray of sunlight on the ruby. "I want it. I want *you*. I have, I think, from the first moment. Caressing that escritoire at the earl's fete. I could only imagine your hands running all over *me*."

"You will then?" He gave the ruby a light tap, trying to control what was happening—*hardening*—behind his trouser close. The future promise of her body closing around his was becoming the loudest thing in his head. "Marry me? Help me raise Kat. Have more children if we're lucky."

She wound her arms around him, tunneling her fingers through his hair and bringing his lips to hers. "Yes." She nipped his bottom lip, then backed way, causing him to follow. "Although, you're missing three words every girl likes to hear."

He pressed his brow to hers, roping his arm around her waist and settling her against him. Letting her feel what she was doing to him. "Francine Shaw, if I adored you *less*, I'd be able to say more. Say it better. I love you quite madly and without hope of recovery. I only know I want you more than I've ever wanted anything in this life."

"Yes, then," she whispered and pulled him into another sinking kiss. "I will marry you. Because I love you, too. Madly. If the easel arrives by Thursday, that is. If not, all bets are off."

He laughed, his heart breaking. But for the first time, in a good way. "Happy Christmas, my sweet viscountess."

Epilogue

Where a fantastically happy couple make big decisions

Ten Months Later
Derbyshire

Franny took a step back, tilting her head and squinting. "I think the darker shade works. Kat wanted a color close to a bluebell. This is close to a bluebell, isn't it?"

Chance lowered the paintbrush, catching his bottom lip between his teeth. "Hmm..."

Her stomach clenched, heat traveling directly to its chosen spot between her thighs.

Her gaze roved the length of her husband and back. Light hit him just so, perfect for sketching if she'd had her supplies handy. He was dressed for the country in a pair of form-fitting buckskins and a worn linen shirt that clung deliciously to his shoulders and back. Wellingtons polished to a high gloss. He'd been working around the estate the past year, and his body had gotten more muscular if that was possible.

Her need grew with every moment she spent with him. Her love. They were trying for a baby. Still newlyweds, in a sense. Chance had returned from London this morning, so they'd not been able to try for *five* nights. The longest they'd ever gone. "I suppose it works," he said, so earnest it made her heart ache. "But we could try the lighter, too. Or maybe use it on the window frames."

Their adopted daughter, Kat, wanted a blue bedchamber for her seventh birthday. They'd decided to redecorate as a surprise while she spent the day shopping in the village with Ada. Chance had picked the task over the quick romp they both desperately desired, which made Franny love him more. He placed his family's happiness above everything else. Above his own. Adoration he freely showed his girls every day.

"Wait until she finds out about the kitten. I can't wait to give him to her."

"You're spoiling her, Remy."

Shrugging happily, he tapped the windowpane with his brush. His gaze tracked a man galloping a black bay across the fields. "Why is Xander Macauley here again?"

Franny came to stand beside him, snaking her arm through his and leaning into his side. He turned slightly to kiss the crown of her head. He smelled wonderful. Leather and the crisp scent of wood, scents that were Chance's own. His furniture was selling like mad, although the *ton* still had no idea Viscount Remington had a side business. He'd yet to have a desk placed in Carlton House, though the king had expressed interest in having one at Windsor Castle, which Franny assured Chance was even better. "He's having woman troubles, or so he implied. Who was the last one? An actress?"

"Opera singer. Italian, I believe," Chance murmured, drawing his wife close and nuzzling the side of her neck. "Coincidental timing, isn't it? When the Duke of Leighton, his new duchess, and sisters are arriving tomorrow. And Arthur, finally, has agreed to stay until the summer."

Franny watched Macauley halt his mount and slide from the saddle, a towering beast of a man. She liked him. He was genuine in a sea of pretenders. Rough around the edges, cynical, demanding. But he'd been a good friend. A sound business partner to her husband. He had love in his eyes waiting to be unleashed. "What does Leighton coming to pay a visit have to do with Xander Macauley?"

Chance chuckled, a sly ripple of sound. He and Macauley were constantly trying to one-up each other. Wagers on billiards, hunting, hazard. Fisticuffs on the lawn. Fencing in the ballroom. Pushes and shoves and outright brawls. It seemed almost brotherly in nature. "He's got his eye on Lady Philippa, though he wishes like hell he didn't. I'm going to seat her right next to him at dinner and watch him squirm."

Franny's lips parted, a gasp shooting free. This *was* news. "Pippa? Leighton's little sister?" She eyed Macauley as he led the horse toward a stable they'd just outfitted with a new roof.

The *ton* would accept Macauley pilfering their ducal coffers about as well as they'd accepted Franny plundering this viscountcy. Society didn't call her the American Enchantress with great affection. "Will the Duchess Society clean him up? Straighten him out? Leighton would never let him marry her as his reputation stands."

Chance tossed the brush into the bucket by his feet and swept her into his arms, his lips seizing hers. *My*, the man could kiss. "Oh, my naïve darling. Desire isn't love. He'll never tell a soul, make an offer, or a move. But he watches her whenever she's in the room. Every *time* she's in the room. I can't believe Leighton hasn't seen it. But when he does, he'll knock Macauley flat on his arse."

"Let's seat them next to each other, let's do. I want to watch what happens."

"That's my girl," he said and kissed his way down her jaw. "Later, after Kat is in bed, you could meet me at my workshop at the edge of the woodland. You can scream as loudly as you'd like. And you know, I'll do anything you ask."

She sighed, her head dropping back. "I did terribly like that one thing you tried the other night. With your fingers *and* your tongue."

"Done," he whispered against her neck.

"I'm happy, Chance." Dipping her head, she burrowed against his chest. "You've made me happy for the first time. I never want to leave you, even for one night. I'm going to London next time. Five days apart was too much."

Chance pulled back until she could see his face. He liked to look into her eyes when he told her he loved her. "Francine Allerton, you're the light of my existence. You and Kat. And now that orange scrap of a kitten. I give thanks every night that you came into my life. You know that, don't you? I feel *lucky*. To the ends of the earth lucky."

She pressed her cheek against the warmth of his chest, his heart beating beneath her ear. "So, you'll sit for me this weekend? I want to try out the oils this time. I've been practicing."

Chance brought her close with a kiss. "My darling viscountess, I'm your subject for life."

THE END

Thank you for reading *The Governess Gamble*!

Interested in reading about Hildy and her sizzling love story with the king of the London underworld, Tobias Streeter? Check out their steamy, banter-filled tale in *The Brazen Bluestocking*. Your Duchess Society membership awaits!

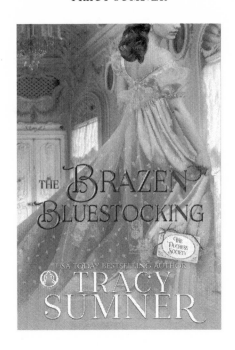

Also by Tracy Sumner

The Duchess Society Series

The Ice Duchess *(Prequel)*

The Brazen Bluestocking

The Scandalous Vixen

The Wicked Wallflower

One Wedding and an Earl

League of Lords Series

The Lady is Trouble

The Rake is Taken

The Duke is Wicked

The Hellion is Tamed

Garrett Brothers Series

Tides of Love

Tides of Passion

Tides of Desire: A Christmas Romance

Southern Heat Series

To Seduce a Rogue

To Desire a Scoundrel: A Christmas Seduction

Standalone Regency romances

Tempting the Scoundrel

Chasing the Duke

About Tracy Sumner

USA Today bestselling and award-winning author Tracy Sumner's storytelling career began when she picked up a historical romance on a college beach trip, and she fondly blames LaVyrle Spencer for her obsession with the genre. She's a recipient of the National Reader's Choice, and her novels have been translated into Dutch, German, Portuguese and Spanish. She lived in New York, Paris and Taipei before finding her way back to the Lowcountry of South Carolina.

When not writing sizzling love stories about feisty heroines and their temperamental-but-entirely-lovable heroes, Tracy enjoys reading, snowboarding, college football (Go Tigers!), yoga, and travel. She loves to hear from romance readers!

Connect with Tracy: www.tracy-sumner.com

facebook.com/Tracysumnerauthor
twitter.com/sumnertrac
instagram.com/tracysumnerromance
bookbub.com/profile/tracy-sumner
amazon.com/Tracy-Sumner/e/B000APFV3G

Made in the USA
Middletown, DE
26 February 2023

25707009R00068